A WILDE PLAYERS DIRTY ROMANCE

USA *Today* Bestselling Authors

A.M. HARGROVE
& TERRI E. LAINE

Published By Wicked Truth Publishing, LLC
Copyright © 2016 A.M. Hargrove and Terri E. Laine
All rights reserved.

This is a work of fiction. Any resemblance to peoples either living
or deceased is purely coincidental. Names, places, and characters
are figments of the author's imagination, or, if real, used
fictitiously.

Cover by Michele Catalano - Creative

Cover photo by Perrywinkle Photography

ISBN-13: 978-1540547729
ISBN: 1540547728

DEDICATION

This one is dedicated to women who love sports and to the hot men who love to play them.

PROLOGUE

Spending the summer in the mountains of Western North Carolina is my favorite thing to do. Living in California puts us so far away from all our relatives. My twin brother, Ryder, and I always look forward to going to my cousins' Fletcher and Chase's every year. My parents do it so we stay close. It was a decision they made when my dad's job took him to the West Coast.

This summer has been different. Ryder is letting me hang out with the guys, and Fletcher's friends are amazing. But there's this one. Mark James. Dark and manly. Or at least I think he's manly. He acts more like a grown-up than the other boys. He wears his hair really cool, too. It's short all over, except it's a bit longer and messy on the top. It hangs over his forehead, drawing attention to his blue-gray eyes. They are large, and beautiful, so clear, yet framed by a ridiculously thick fringe of lashes. And every time I check him out, he's staring openly at me, not even trying to hide it. Just the other day, we were all eating the sandwiches my aunt had prepared, and when I reached to grab the extra-large bag of chips, they accidentally spilled everywhere. His arm brushed against mine as he helped me gather the chips, and the shivers that sped up my back had my head jerking toward him. He didn't utter a word, only slid his teeth over his bottom lip, and his mouth quirked.

Trying to pretend I don't care if he's here or not isn't easy. The last thing I want is for Ryder to know. The teasing would be endless, and I'm not up for that. Knowing him, he'd blabber about my crush to Fletcher, and then Chase, and before I'd know it, I'm sure there'd be a news reporter knocking on the front door.

But my days are numbered. In less than a week, we leave for California. Home. And I won't see Mark until next summer. And that's if we even return next year. I overheard my parents talking. Fletcher will graduate next year, which means he'll be in college playing football. I almost didn't come this summer because of golf. Ryder only came because he was able to play on a baseball summer league team here. Next year will be different for all of us. And that means after this week, I'll never see Mark again.

The day we're leaving, my bags are packed and everyone is hanging around. Mom, Dad, and my aunt and uncle are discussing things in the kitchen, so I decide to hang out on the tire swing outside. The noise of tires on gravel alerts my attention, and I look up to see Mark getting out of his car. He notices me and walks over.

"What are you doing out here? Is Ryder or Fletcher around? Fletcher asked me to meet him here."

I shrug. "I haven't seen either of them in a while. I think they walked out back somewhere."

He nods. "Okay, then."

For a moment we just look at each other. He shoves his hands into his pockets. "I guess I'll go find them."

He starts to walk off.

"Hey, wait up. Do you want some company?"

He shrugs again, so I catch up.

"I hear you are leaving," he finally says.

"Today, actually."

Something feels off. It's weird between us, and I don't know why. We walk in silence until we've made it behind the barn. He uses a hand to shield his eyes as he looks off into the distance.

"Do you see them?" I didn't, but I didn't know what else to say.

"No." He faces me, blocking the sun with his height. I rub my palms on my shorts, suddenly nervous. He licks his lips, and I wish like hell I had the nerve to kiss him.

"Riley."

His eyes are glued to mine, and a strange ache grows in my belly.

"Yes."

"I'm kinda glad Fletcher or Ryder isn't around."

"Why?"

He doesn't speak for the longest time.

"I'm just going to say it."

"What?" I ask.

"All summer." He pauses and he must believe I know how that sentence ends because his eyes continue to bore into me. He shakes his head as if to clear it. "All summer, I've wanted to kiss you and now you're leaving."

"Kiss me?"

My stomach flutters with a gazillion butterflies, because, yeah, when a guy like him says something like that, it's an off-the-charts diary-worthy moment.

"Yes."

His one word answer has me as tongue-tied as I've ever been and I hate myself for it.

"Okay." Now's the time I should be saying things like how much fun I've had hanging with him this summer, and how I hope we can talk, blah, blah, blah. But no. It's as if someone has duct taped my mouth shut.

He takes my hand in his.

"I've wanted this since I first saw you, since the beginning."

Before I know what's happened, warm, soft lips touch mine and then his tongue pushes its way into my mouth. Honestly, I want to curl into him and beg him to come home with me. I've been kissed before, but never, ever, like this. He curves his tongue around mine, and it seems as though he's discovering as many secrets as I am. His hand slips into my hair, and I do the same to him.

Our bodies are touching in all the right places, leaving no space between us for even a tiny bit of air to seep in. I feel him down in the marrow of my bones.

"Riley." I hear my brother's voice out in the distance.

The spell having been broken, we jerk apart, but there is something in his expression I can't read, longing, wistfulness, or maybe I'm just misplacing my own feelings.

Then Ryder's there, and the moment is lost.

"Mom says it's time to go."

There's an awkward moment when Ryder glances between the two of us trying to puzzle out what's going on.

Mark is quick with an explanation. "We were looking for you guys," he says to my brother.

"We were," I agree.

Ryder's eyes narrow, but Mark takes the lead and heads back. I walk next to Ryder, but thankfully he doesn't ask any questions. When we arrive, Mom waves Ryder inside to help get our bags. I'm left outside with Mark.

"I wish—"

I don't waste time. If this is it, I want more. Cutting him off, I quickly press my lips to his one last time. Then I back away, leaving him standing there with a dazed expression on his face. But he's done the same to me.

Mark James has marked me, and from this moment on, I will never be the same again. But even though

5

we've seen each other every year after that kiss, that special moment is lost to us. He's had a girlfriend or I've had a boyfriend. He's gone off to college, and I've gone to another. Then we weren't kids anymore. So secretly, I've always wondered *what-if* with no hope of ever finding out the answer to that question.

RILEY

ark glances at me as Gina lets out a long and loud moan. Can this get any more embarrassing? The fact that I've been crushing on Mark for years is bad enough. But Ryder upstairs fucking his fiancée, and by the sounds of it, doing quite a bang-up job, is even worse.

Now I'm questioning my choice to live with my brother, an ace MLB pitcher. He has a huge condo in downtown Charlotte. You'd think the sound wouldn't carry. Either the walls are super thin or they are super loud. I'd like to think the former. As that last thought leaves my mind, my brother lets out the longest groan.

"What the hell are they doing up there?" I mutter.

"I don't know, but I sure as hell would like to find out," Mark says, as he adjusts his pants. We're standing next to the island in the kitchen as we debate whether or not he can be my stand-in caddie for a charity golf event

I have coming up. My former caddie resigned at the end of the season, and I have yet to find a replacement. Admittedly, I'm desperate. I can't help but stare at the bulge left of center of his crotch. It makes me squirm. All thoughts of the LPGA have flown from my mind.

"Hey, eyes up here, Eagle."

Being caught red-handed isn't something I'm proud of, especially with that smirk on his face. But damn, it's been a while since I've had any, and Mark is smokin' hot. Not only a head taller than me, with dark hair and eyes that can't decide if they're blue or gray, he's beyond sexy—even more so than when we were teenagers. But his strong jaw and full pouty lips have always begged to be kissed. I do as he says, but not quickly. I take my time, letting my eyes do a little roaming from his crotch to neck as I think about what I'd want him to do to me. Crossing my legs, my attempt to ease the ache between them fails.

"What's the problem?" he asks.

Gina and Ryder moan in unison, and then yell some unintelligible crap. This is too much for any sexually active—or inactive as in my case—and horny as hell woman to bear. One glance at Mark is all it takes and he grabs a fistful of my shirt. His mouth crashes onto mine, and I push him against the island, indicating I'm all in. The kiss is heated, demanding, and potent. Lust fires my veins, and there's only one ending I have in mind. It's a hard and fast fuck. I hope he's into this, because if not, I'm going to have to excuse myself and take a trip to my bedroom for some vibrator time.

When his hands latch on to my hips and push my pants down, I figure we're on the same page. In the background, Gina and Ryder sound like they're at a rodeo riding the bull, but I want to ride the reverse pony on Mark. Before this gets any further, I grab my pants and pull them back up.

"Come with me."

"I was hoping to," he says.

"Such a comedian. Hurry."

We run up the stairs, and I push him inside the doorway of my room. Up here we get the full impact of the Gina-Ryder effect.

"Christ. Are they always like this?" he asks.

"I don't know. I'm gone so much, and when I'm here, I put on my sound machine."

"I've never heard anything like it."

Grabbing the waist of his jeans, I unbutton and unzip them. Tugging them down at light speed, I grab his stiff cock, loving the velvety firmness of it. Not giving it a second thought, I drop to my knees and wrap my lips around it as I pull his length into my mouth. His deep moans spur me on to take him in further. But he pulls me off and strips off my pants and thong. He's aggressive as he pushes me onto the edge of the bed and plants my feet there as he spreads me wide.

"Riley, I—"

"Don't talk. Just do it." Wouldn't Nike be proud of me now?

Without further urging from me, his mouth is gentle as he runs his wet tongue—and, oh, what a tongue it is—along my slit, and I nearly buck off the bed. His hand presses me back down, keeping me steady, as he works over my open pussy. He does this little twirly thing while his finger seems to locate some secret hidden places inside me, and the orgasm that hovers over me suddenly decides to present itself in full force.

Unfortunately for Mark, my thighs clamp together, and I may or may not have squished his head a bit. One thing I did do was moan very loudly. Probably loud enough to rival Gina and Ryder. They don't notice, and from the sounds of it, they're still at it like two hounds chasing a fox.

Mark stands and grabs his wallet out of his pants pocket. He finds a condom and holds it up. "Are you in for this, too?"

"Oh, hell yeah." No way would I miss out on the grand finale.

My eager eyes watch him as he rolls on the latex, and it's super hot. But what he does next is even hotter. He grabs his cocks and strokes himself, up and down, making me swallow as drool threatens to run out of my mouth.

"Jesus, that's hot," I say.

"Not compared to what I'm looking at."

We stare at each other for a while until I say, "You either need to do something or I'm going to have to take things into my own hand."

His teeth glide over his lower lip, and a raspy chuckle escapes from him right after the headboard from Ryder's room starts banging on the wall, accompanied by some *ughs* and *ahhs*.

"Think you can rival that?" I challenge.

"Only one way to find out."

He crawls onto the bed and pushes me back. Then my legs end up on his shoulders as his tip hovers at my opening. He slides his cock around, up and down, and pushes it in, slowly. Then backs out. He repeats, and I'm hypnotized by his actions. The routine is heating my veins, igniting my blood on fire. When he finally pushes in and is seated deep, he pulls out, and then slams back in, hard and fast, ripping the breath right out of me. Heart thumping in my throat, nails scoring his shoulders, I hang on for the ride of my life. And what a ride it is. My climax sends me soaring and screaming for joy. But he's not done. He flips me like a flapjack and continues to pound into me, never breaking stride. I'm stretched out, flat on my stomach, one of his arms under my hips as he pumps into me. I arch my back with each thrust, accepting what he's willing to give.

His warm breath is on my neck, followed by his lips and tongue, and tremors vibrate up and down my spine. Every nerve ending tingles, and I know I'm going to come again. His hand migrates to my core, and his thumb places a gentle pressure on my clit. That's all it takes to eke another orgasm out of me. My inner muscles clench, and I can feel him pulsate inside of me as he groans out his own climax.

When we finish, he rolls me over and situates me on top of him. Our mouths press together in scorching kisses, and we have a nice little make-out session. His scruff rubs my cheeks tender in a few spots, and it makes me giggle.

"What?"

"I didn't think we'd end up doing this today," I admit.

"Me neither. But I have to say, I'm pretty damn happy about it."

"Yeah?"

"Yeah. What about you?" he asks.

"I'm okay with it."

"Okay with it? Hmm. That doesn't sound too good to me."

"No, it's good." I don't want to give everything away here. If he knows that I've been crushing on him, then he'll have the upper hand, and that won't work at all. Besides, if he's going to work for me, I have to maintain some kind of authority here.

"Good?" he repeats.

Now he sounds hurt, and that's not what I intended.

"It was really good."

"I get the feeling you're not okay with this. And you can be honest with me," he says.

"That's not it." How can I say this? "Here's the deal. If you come work for me, then we have to be professional."

He bursts out laughing. "Is that what this is all about?"

"Yeah." But it kind of pisses me off. "And it's not funny."

"Your attitude about it is. Riley, I'm a grown man. To say I can't act professional is ridiculous."

"You can't say that. I've seen people much older than you walk away from situations because of crazy things."

He nods. "You're right. But I would hope you and I could be bigger people."

"I would hope that, too."

A banging on the door interrupts us. "Ri, is that you?" Ryder asks.

"Who else would be in my room?" I can't help the snarky reply that comes out of my mouth.

"Who's in there with you?"

"Hey, since when did that become any of your business?" I retort.

"Since I want to make sure you're okay."

"Seriously, you are not asking me that."

"Yeah, I am."

"Ryder, go back to your room."

"I can't believe him," I mumble to Mark.

"He's only being a good brother."

"Is that Mark?" Ryder asks.

"Oh, my, God! Are you standing out there listening?"

"Where do you think I am? In the kitchen?"

Jumping out of bed, I throw on my clothes and yank the door open. "I can't believe you. You're an ass. That's the stupidest thing you've ever done."

He pushes his way into the room and looks at Mark, who barely had time to cover himself with a sheet. "Hey, man."

"What the hell is this? Are you gonna bring him a cup of coffee now?" I ask. "Get out of here." He gives me a shitty little grin and leaves, and I slam the door behind him.

I turn to Mark, and he sits there with an expectant look on his face. "What?" I ask.

"Coffee would be great, Eagle."

I grab a pillow within reach and throw it at him before stomping out of the room. His laughter follows me down the stairs. *Coffee my ass*. He can get his own damn coffee. If anyone gets coffee in bed, it's gonna be me, dammit.

MARK

My *Eagle has landed*, I think as I watch Riley's sweet ass leave the room. Taller than most women I've dated, she's still leaner than the others with muscle from her athleticism, which makes her sexy as fuck. Add to that, dark hair that cascades down her back like a waterfall. Jerking off to thoughts of her haven't compared to the real thing. And she's starred in many of my dreams over the years. I never thought in a million years to be here. We'd kissed once so long ago, but the memory never faded into obscurity.

As small as the world is, it never occurred to me, with her and her family living in California, that she would move back here when she was old enough to do so.

The spooked look in Riley's eyes before she left has me getting dressed. Gina's out in the hallway with Ryder when I pass through the door.

"So, you finally did it," Gina, my first ever ex-girlfriend and one of my current best friends, says.

And I think of how complicated this whole thing is. Gina and I lost our virginities to each other when we were in high school, but broke up soon after. Her best friend, Cassie, is married to my best friend, Fletcher Wilde, a star quarterback in the NFL, who is also Ryder and Riley's cousin.

"Don't go there," I warn.

Ryder starts to say something, and I think about punching him. Hell, I owe him one. But Gina stops him and walks over to me. Placing both hands on my shoulders, she says, "Remember, don't smother her. Give the girl some space. She's like me."

She winks, and I'm annoyed. "We're not in high school anymore. I can handle myself."

Gina's not offended by my brusqueness, and it shows how well she knows me.

"Go get her," Gina whispers.

My annoyance is wiped away. I smile as I head down the stairs. Riley is in the kitchen slamming cabinets and muttering to herself.

"Hey," I say, taking her arm when I reach her. She stops. "Let's not get weird, okay. We're two consenting adults. We had some fun. We got it out of our system."

But since she's so far from out of my system, I have to force the lie out.

"Good." She breathes out and says, "Good, good," again on another exhale. "This could never work. We'll have to practice together. No time to think about sex, with you." She's talking more to herself as she searches in vain for a mug she finally finds. Clearly, she's rattled because of what we did. "And then the week of the event, I need to be focused on my game and the little kids from the Make-A-Wish Foundation we're doing this for."

Feeling the need to calm her, I casually say, "Sounds good."

"Whew." She blows out another breath.

I can't help but have my ego bruised. She's so eager to get rid of me. Maybe Gina is right and they are a lot alike. Gina had broken my heart way back when. I'll never know if it was love or infatuation because I love her now. I'm just not in love with her. Still, she'd been the girl that got away. And that will always sting. As of right now, I'm not sure I'm ready for any commitments, especially with losing my job and wondering what's next.

"So, are you going to give me a shot?"

Panic fills her eyes, and she quickly asks, "At being my caddie?"

"What else?"

"Yeah, I need to see if I can get some tee times so we can get some practice time in."

"Sure. I guess I should leave."

What I really want is for her to ask me to stay, but she doesn't. The taste of her is still on my tongue, and I hate that we went at it so fast. I didn't get enough time with her tight little breasts and her amazing ass.

"It's probably a good thing," she murmurs.

I don't beg because with a girl like Riley that

17

wouldn't work. There's also no need to comment again about what we did and how good it was for me. There's so much regret in her ideas, my ego has taken a beating next to her *it was good* comment.

Without ceremony, I'm out. The drive back to Asheville is long and brutal. I may not have a job, but I didn't think driving two hours to Charlotte to meet with her would end so soon. Usually, I date women a while before by mutual agreement we call it quits. Will I ever find the one?

Sighing, I give my car the verbal command to call Fletcher. I've never been one to fuck and tell, but if I don't call him, he'll hear it from Gina and call to give me shit anyway.

"Mark, don't you sleep in these days?" he answers.

"Har-fucking-har," I say. Just because I'm financially sound without my job, doesn't mean that I enjoy being jobless. "And I hear you might become a Cowgirl."

I'm talking about the speculation of his potential trade to Dallas, though I know better. He's doing his best to get traded to the Carolina's team.

"Damn, man, that's harsh. And don't say that around Cassidy. She's hoping for a trade to the Panthers so we can spend more time in Waynesville. Besides, I was kidding with you. What's up?"

There's no easy way to say it, so I just do.

"I fucked Riley."

Silence.

"Look, Gina and Ryder were there. They know. You

would have found out."

"It's not like it's my business," he says.

"I would agree, but she's your cousin, etc., etc."

"So—"

"Nothing, man. It was a one-time deal. She's like Gina's clone or something."

I hate the bitter pill I have to swallow.

"Gina did settle down," he counters.

"Exactly, and not with me. Not that I wanted to. But the point is, Riley's like Gina. She'll never be mine, and I'm moving on."

Okay, that last bit might have sounded true to my own ears if I didn't know how I truly felt.

"Whatever you say."

"Yeah, so now you know," I say. "And I have to go. I'm driving and shouldn't be on the phone."

It may be a fact, but we know it's an excuse.

"Mark?"

"What?" I want this conversation to end and pretend it didn't happen.

"Maybe this time don't just walk away. If this is what you want, fight for her."

His words circle in my head as I drive home. When Gina broke things off, she had a fucking checklist for the reasons why we were better off as friends. She'd made sense. I didn't much argue as pride held together some of my self-respect. Had I truly not fought for Gina? If I had, would things be different? I shake that thought away because I'm sure it wouldn't be. She'd been right.

We are better off as friends. But what about Riley?

To put it in perspective, I think about the women I've dated. None have ever clicked. Yet, there's something about Riley. Something that makes me look for her whenever I'm at a Wilde family affair and I know she's in town.

At home, I pour myself some orange juice and consider pouring a shot instead. Drinking won't solve anything. Thank goodness I don't because a call I've been expecting comes through.

"Mark James?"

"This is he."

"Hi, it's Ben Rhoades."

Ben's the head of an investment firm in Charleston, South Carolina that's been courting me for years. Somehow they heard about the dissolution of the firm I was with and contacted me.

"Mr. Rhoades."

He laughs. "Don't call me that. It makes me feel like my father. Call me Ben."

"Ben, then."

There is only a short pause before he gets down to business.

"Mark, I make myself aware of my competition, and your name has crossed the lips of many in the business. And that's big, especially since we're not Wall Street guys."

"You were."

"Were," he says.

"And you came back home."

"And you never left."

"Touché," I say.

"I am impressed by what I hear about you, and I respect your work. Obviously, we would need to work out all the details, but I'm prepared to offer you an opportunity to set up and run a satellite office for us in Charlotte."

Rhoades Investment has made a name for themselves. They're well respected, and it's an opportunity I have to consider.

"And if I were interested?" I ask.

"It would mean you would come down for a formal interview. You would meet with my father and me, along with other key personnel. If everything goes well and you agree to come on board, you would need to spend some time in our office here in Charleston to get to know how our operation runs. Of course, we would put you up here in the city for the duration of your stay. Then you could work remotely from your house while we scout for a location and start the hiring process in Charlotte."

Everything sounds good. Being in charge and starting a business as if it were new appeals to me. Still, I can't just jump at the first opportunity.

"I'll need to think about it."

"I wouldn't expect less. How about we schedule time for you to at least come down and talk to us? I would hate for you to make a decision without talking to us first."

"Sounds fair."

Then I remember Riley and agreeing to be her caddie. "Why don't you give me some times and I'll check my schedule?"

Credit to him for not pointing out the obvious, like shouldn't all my time be free since I'm not working?

"Good. I look forward to meeting you, Mark."

"You, too, Ben."

It's not long before several proposed days and times appear in my inbox on my phone. As much as I want to ignore Riley until she calls me, I'll have to get in touch with her before tomorrow. I can't let too much time pass before I answer Ben, especially if I want to look as though I'm seriously considering his offer.

RILEY

Why the hell does he have to be so damn sexy and great in the sack, too? It's all I can think of and I need to wipe that out of my head so I can think golf. *Golf. Did you hear that, Riley? You have an event coming up, and your short game sucks right now. You need to figure out your putting, and fast.*

After setting up a ton of tee times, I text Mark and ask him when he can be here. The smart-ass wants to know if it's okay if he stays at Ryder's. Did you hear that? Not at my place, but at Ryder's. Ugh.

"Ryder? You around?" I yell.

"Yeah, why?"

"Can Mark stay here? He's going to be my caddie."

Now my brother goes and pisses me off. He laughs at my question. Then he asks, "Why you asking me? Seems to me you had that sharing a bed thing all figured out already."

"You know what? You're a douche."

"What'd I say now?" Then I hear him ask Gina as I stomp up the stairs to my room, "What'd I do?"

"Why are men so damn clueless?" I grumble to myself as I text Mark back and add the tee times so he knows when to be back here. We start practice tomorrow, but I'm headed to the course today to hit some balls. My swing needs to be adjusted, so I have a long session with my coach in an hour. It would be nice to have my new caddie here for that, but that would be a bit too much to ask.

Thirty minutes into our session and Randy, my coach, says, "What the hell is wrong with you? You're acting like a hair twirler."

"A what?"

"A hair twirler. That's what I call my daughter when she's playing soccer and she's more interested in the boys watching her than she is in the game."

I want to deck him with my driver. "I am not."

"Then explain why every ball you hit is either a slice or a fade. And beyond that, you average around two hundred and fifty yards on your drives. You're barely hitting the two hundred mark. Check your tracker if you don't believe me. But don't worry. I have it all on the GoPro." He taps the tiny camera mounted to the golf bag he uses to analyze my swing. I can't argue with a thing he's said. My swing is off. Everything's off, and it's because of Mark and the romp in the sack we had.

Randy won't let it go. "So? Are you seeing that PGA guy again? What's his name?"

"No, I'm not seeing him." And he knows damn well what his name is.

"Then who is it? Rickie Fowler?"

"Shut up. Rickie has a girlfriend. Everybody knows that," I say as I get ready to take another swing.

When I finish, he says, "A little better. Is it Jordan Speith?"

"No! He has a serious girlfriend, too. But I will say if his caddie weren't married, I might be digging on him." I tee up and swing again.

"Hmm. You rotated your hand on the club. Here." He adjusts my grip and says, "This is where you're supposed to be. Why'd you change?"

Why did I change? "Guess I wasn't paying attention."

"Hair twirling. Is it Rory McIlroy? Last I heard he was a free agent."

"I'm not hair twirling," I insist, but in reality, he's right. And it's all Mark and his talented cock's fault. "I think you're wrong about Rory. Besides, he lives too far away."

"Planes, trains, and automobiles."

After about a hundred more balls, Randy announces I'm getting closer to my old self. "That's more like the Riley I used to see out here. Now, give me a couple hundred balls like that."

"Hand me a water, please."

I'm well into another bucket when he says, "Whoa, whoa, you're over rotating your hips." He gets behind

25

me and demonstrates. I'm off again until he stops me with a, "Watch that back swing. You're not trying to kill anyone. The ball isn't back there, Ri. Your power is in the swing through. Stop a minute."

I step back and guzzle down a water. "Here." He hands me a protein bar. While I eat, he talks.

"Think of this. When you hammer in a nail, you don't take the hammer back with all your might, do you?"

"No."

"That's how you need to think of your driver."

He's right.

"I'm noticing here that you're acting like you want to kill something with it, namely the ball. That's why you've been so sloppy. Check it out." He hits replay on the GoPro and shows me my errors on my back swing.

"Jeez, I look like a madwoman."

"Just tame it a little. You'll have way more control when you convert. But you know that already. A mistake that's easily corrected."

I finish eating my bar, and he says, "Let's switch to a 5 wood."

After another thousand balls, he checks the clock and says it's time to call it quits. I've practiced for seven hours.

"You playing tomorrow?" he asks.

"Yes, with my substitute caddie. I need to break him in." In more ways than one.

"Good. Let me know how it goes. You need to play

thirty-six holes. At a minimum."

I promise to play at least that many, and we part ways. Heading to the ladies' locker room, I lock up my clubs and shoes and then head for home. I walk in and hear voices. Ryder must have company. But I'm surprised to see who's sitting there.

"How was your practice?" Mark asks.

Miss McGrumpy returns, because all the time I spent hitting balls pisses me off.

"Dandy. I couldn't hit worth a shit. My coach was all over my ass for it. I can't even tell you how many balls I hit. Seven hours' worth, that's how many." He doesn't deserve my snarky attitude at all, but whatever.

"Damn, that's a lot of balls."

"Tell me. I'm the one with the sore arms," I blast back.

Then Ryder says, "Yeah, but you love it."

My mouth runs away from me. "Um, unlike the gods of the baseball diamonds, there are no restrictions on how many swings I can take per day. So I don't *love* it all the time, brother."

"Whoa, excuse me. Someone is certainly in a bad mood today," Ryder says.

"You would be, too."

"So, can I fix you something to eat? Drink?" Mark asks. I'm sure he's only trying to defray the tension in the room. And now I feel like a bitch, especially since he drove all the way back here to help me out.

"A drink would be great, and thanks. Sorry for being

27

so snappy, Ryder."

"No worries, sis. I get it. All days can't be great out there."

Falling back on the couch, I put my feet on the coffee table and feel the tension drain. "I'm so glad the heat is gone. If this would've been August—ugh. It really would've sucked."

Gina strolls into the room and asks if we want to go to dinner. Ryder jumps up and announces he'll treat. I'm exhausted, but I'll look like super bitch if I don't go.

"Let me change out of these clothes." I head to my room and do a quick wardrobe redo. When I'm up there, I decide a brief shower might wake me up. Thirty minutes later, I'm ready to go.

They're all waiting on me when I get downstairs. "Sorry, I needed to shower. So, where are we headed?"

Gina announces there's this new place she's been dying to try—one of those bistro-type places that also offers small plates.

"Um, Gina, do you know who you're marrying? He can eat enough for twenty."

"I cannot," Ryder argues.

My only response is a raised brow. We go to the new place, and after Ryder sees the menu, he decides he needs three entrees.

"Told ya," I say. "The man with a bottomless pit for a stomach."

Mark chuckles. "Good thing you don't put on weight, dude."

Ryder pats his stomach and says, "I watch what I eat and work out a lot."

I almost spit out my wine. "You may work out a lot, but the only watching about what you eat is the way you put it in your mouth."

Everyone laughs, even Ryder. We finish ordering our food, and Mark tells us about his job offer. I have a brief panic attack until he says he's still going to caddie for me.

"It's only an interview, so don't worry, Eagle."

"But this is super important to me. It started out for a young girl with cancer, and a bunch of pros have joined in on this. It's turned into a big fundraiser—much bigger than originally planned. That's why it's so critical for me to do well, which is why I need you on board one hundred percent."

Ryder and Gina are squirming now, so maybe it's best if we talk about this later. "Look, we have a lot to talk about, and I probably haven't shared some things with you that I need to, so let's discuss this when we get home," I suggest.

"Good idea," Mark says. Dinner ultimately ends, and when we get home, I pull Mark into the small den where Ryder has a large screen TV set up specifically for movies. This is the perfect place for a private chat with him.

"So, this charity golf match has gotten so much attention from the LPGA and the PGA, it's now become a huge event. There'll be other sick kids there, along with their parents, and a total of eighteen golfers. Each kid will rotate and get to play with each golfer. So it's a pretty cool deal. Not to mention some of the sponsors are ponying up large amounts, upwards of five hundred thousand dollars. The money will be divided among each of the kids, with bonuses paid out to the winning male and female golfers. The idea is for the golfers then to donate their winnings to Make-A-Wish. It stands to pull in a ton for these kids."

"I had no idea." Mark rubs his chin.

"Yeah, and that's my fault. I didn't tell you. Honestly, I didn't get all the information until the other day."

"So, what do you need from me?" he asks.

"I need you one hundred ten percent. I have to teach you *my* golf game. I know you understand golf, but you don't understand how I play it. That's why the next week is crucial because that's all the time we'll have to practice before the event."

He grabs my hand and says, "I'm there."

"But the job interview."

"I'll figure it out. There has to be something. It's only a couple of hours. Maybe I can meet them at night."

I chew on the inside of my mouth. He's not my employee, so it's not fair to make demands of him. "I will pay you for this. If I haven't made this clear, I'm not expecting you to do this for free."

He wears an insulted expression. "I won't do it if you pay me. That is the most ludicrous thing I've ever heard."

"It's taking over a week out of your time. Of course, I'll pay you, and it's not ludicrous. I can afford it, Mark. If you are unaware, I'm one of the top LPGA players."

"Eagle, I am aware." Now he looks at me as though I'm stupid. And I am. Mark is astute. He probably knows all my stats, too.

"Okay, so what do we do?"

"I'll figure something out. Even if I have an evening meeting, I'll be ready to work with you by the morning. It'll work, Riley. I promise."

"You're sure? Because if this doesn't work, I need to make other arrangements, and fast."

"I'm sure. Now stop acting weird toward me. Like we haven't slept together," he says.

"I'm not acting weird."

"Yes, you are."

"Nah, I'm not. I'm tired is all."

"Come on, Riley. I'm not stupid, nor am I blind."

What am I supposed to say now?

"Mark, honestly, it's fine. I'm fine. We're fine."

"You're sure?"

"Totally. It was a grueling day. Randy hasn't put me through a session like that in a while."

"Randy?" he asks suspiciously.

"My coach." My ego is cheering. He sounds a little possessive of me.

"Oh. And how old is this Randy?"

"Why? You jealous?"

He shrugs. "Maybe."

"Don't be. He's married with three kids."

"Oh." His blue-gray eyes dig deep holes into my own, punching the air right out of me. Fuck. Then, wouldn't you know, Gina starts moaning. For the love of God. I stare at the ceiling, and the situation is too comical for me to ignore. Mark must agree because we both burst out laughing.

But it doesn't last long. Heat rolls off him as his fingers skim across my cheek.

"Do you have any idea how gorgeous you are?"

Words escape me, but his mouth is so close, too close, so I grab his arms and pull him toward me. Only he stops me.

"I don't want any more weirdness between us."

"I can handle it."

"I don't think you can." He dislodges my hands and starts to move toward the door.

"Mark, wait."

"Riley, we're two consenting adults, and if we do this again, you can't be acting like a lunatic the way you did before. I'm way past that shit. Tell me now or I'm out this door."

MARK

Her hand latches on to my cock in response.

"No crazy, I promise."

I seal her mouth with mine, putting a halt to any further conversation. She tastes sweet like the chocolate and strawberry dessert she ate. Tangling her tongue with mine, I score my fingers down her back until I reach her ass. I cup it and lift. She's all lean muscle and soft curves. I step backward, forcing her against the wall as her legs wrap around me.

The door opens behind us, and Gina stumbles in.

"My eyes, my eyes." Gina claws at her face, while I groan.

Sadly, I let Riley down and face my now former friend.

"I could have sworn you and Ryder were fucking like rabbits upstairs," I say.

Gina, never having shame, freely admits what they'd been up to. "We were or he tried. But I thought it was rude. So I came down to see if you guys wanted to watch a movie."

"Sure," Riley says.

"No," I growl at the same time.

I glare at Riley. "Unbelievable."

"They're leaving in the morning, and they'll be gone for a while," Riley adds.

Grinding my teeth, I throw up my hands and head for the door. Half-jokingly, I say to Gina, "You used to be one of my best friends."

"Mark," she calls out, but I make for the room Riley had designated for my use earlier that day.

I might have closed the door a little loudly, but my dick could penetrate steel. If she expects me to watch a movie, I will have to either calm the fuck down or rub one out right quick.

The attached bath becomes my destination, but I stop when the door opens.

"Sorry," Riley all but whispers. She leans her back on the door with her hands behind her. "Maybe we could do both."

She speaks like our conversation in the other room hadn't ended.

Pushing off, she strides for me with purposeful steps. Once she's in front of me, she loops her arms around my neck and tugs me forward. I could resist, but I don't. I accept her kiss. "I want you."

There's no game in her statement. She's blunt, and I like it.

"Hard and fast?" I ask.

She nods.

The woman before me is so irresistible I have to grab my dick before it rips through my pants.

"Take off your clothes, because if I do it, I'm liable to destroy them."

Her giggle is the sexiest sound in the world. My dick becomes a rocket launcher ready to shoot off inside her.

"Want a show, do ya?"

Slowly, I let my head tilt up and down. I lick my lips as she starts with her pants. Her pussy is the prettiest I've ever laid eyes on.

"I hope you locked the door. Otherwise, Gina is going to come looking for you because you're taking too long trying to tease me."

She has no problem giving as good as she gets.

"I just like the look on your face, like you're ready to bite me."

Damn, this woman. If she only knew.

"Oh, I'm ready to bite something if you don't hurry it up."

Her infectious laugh makes my balls grow tighter. Any more and I will be able to sing soprano.

She shimmies out of her pants, and she's wearing what appears to be the smallest amount of black material that could cover her. I'm going to nut in my jeans if I don't get inside her soon. Then she's out of her top, and damn her for not wearing a bra. The back of my throat begins to vibrate with sound. Her small breasts are high and round with rosy nipples that beg to be sucked. I hadn't had a chance earlier to really get a good look at them. But there's not enough time to appreciate them with my cock's detonation countdown engaged. Still, I want more.

"Turn around and brace your hands on the edge of the dresser."

Without question, she does what I ask and stares at me with mischief through the mirror.

It's my turn for the show. Slowly, with as much patience as I can muster, I unfasten my belt after procuring a foil packet from my wallet. Everything pools at my feet, and I take my sweet time rolling the condom on. At the base, I fist myself.

"Do you like to play games, Riley?" She nods her head, making me consider telling her to get on her knees. Only if she does that, I'll come like a preteen boy having his first wet dream. "I know some games, too. I'm glad you kept your heels on."

Pulling her hips back, she's at the perfect angle for me to thrust inside her wet folds. Her pussy is tight, and I have to hold her there or risk embarrassing myself. She's having trouble, too. I watch her knuckles go white while she grips the edge tighter.

"Maybe I should stay like this," I tease.

She wiggles in protest. Something comes over me, and I tap the fleshy part of her ass. And for a second, her walls clamp down on me, letting me know she liked that.

"Stop moving or I will," I command.

"I don't think you can," she challenges.

As much as I want to be inside her, I pull out and step back. She turns around and glares at me. Taking my dick in my hand, I start to jerk off, showing her exactly who's in charge. She says nothing, only sucks two fingers into her mouth before spearing herself with them in and out. *Fuck. Me*.

Challenge made and accepted. Neither of us is willing to beg. She ups the ante by using her other hand to pull one of her nipples taut. I'm giving her a show, too. I've hit the sweet part of my rhythm as my hand slides effortlessly up and down my shaft, though I wish it were her pussy closing around my cock.

"Fine," she shouts.

Stalking forward, she shoves me back onto the bed. Then she does the hottest fucking thing ever.

Climbing me like I'm Mount Everest, she hikes herself up my peak, holding my dick straight up to impale herself on it. She's wet, and I reach up wanting to palm her breast. I consider sitting up so I can claim one of them in my mouth.

Only she swivels around, reverse cowgirl style, and rides me like I'm a fucking mustang on the plains of the Wild West. The friction she creates has me on the verge of erupting so hard, I'll probably burst the condom. I place a firm hand on her hip, needing to control the pace. Bucking into her a few times, I decide I want more. I sit up and take a fist full of her hair to expose her throat. Kissing my way to her mouth, I slide my hand from her hip to her clit, circling it until she's begging, saying my name over and over.

There's a knock on the door, and I could give two shits who's on the other side. I reverse our positions, leaving her bent at the waist. Her upper half is pressed into the mattress, and my hand cradling her center keeps her ass high in the air. Her legs are weak, but I'm nowhere near done. I thrust into her hard, making her fist the sheets.

"Should we start the movie without you guys?" Gina calls through the door.

I can almost hear the mirth in her voice, but I remove all thoughts of Gina out of my mind so I can focus on the woman before me.

"What do you say?" I ask, applying pressure on Riley's clit then backing off.

"Yes, yes, yes," she cries.

Her pussy closes around my dick like a cave-in. And no matter how much I wanted to play longer, that sets me off like a rocket into space. A couple more thrusts before I'm falling face-first onto the bed, rolling in time so that Riley's on top of me, with me on my back.

"Fuck me," I grunt.

My legs are Jell-O, and my dick starts to soften inside her. As much as I want to remain where it's wet and warm, if I don't pull out, wearing the condom will have been useless.

I grip the end and take myself out of her.

"And I liked you there," she says in protest.

"Me, too. But something tells me that pushing a stroller on the golf course isn't the latest craze on the LPGA tour."

Her laugh is soft. She's so strong, but in that moment, she seems almost vulnerable.

"We should probably clean up and go watch the movie," she suggests.

"We could or we could stay here."

Soft lips land on my cheek, and she kisses me there. "As much as I want to, I think Gina is going to miss us. She won't say it, but I think staying in New York for a while is going to be lonely for her."

She's right on all counts. There was a time when I would have done anything for Gina. And now she has someone else to fill that role. And so tonight, I'll pass that torch.

After a few minutes, we go to clean up. It's a damn shame when she gets dressed. I like looking at her naked with soft, drowsy eyes because I've taken care of her pleasure.

When we finally make our way into the living room, Riley drapes herself across my lap. It's a wonder how well she fits there as if we were made for each other. She's so comfortable, she lays her head on my chest. Needing to touch her, I rub circles on her back as we watch the movie we all compromised on. It's a romantic one where the hero is a bull rider. But even that can't keep my eyes open. At some point, I dose off. Riley has to wake me up when it's over.

Gina coaxes Ryder awake in the background. "Come on, Cowboy. Let's go up to bed."

"Night," Riley says.

I could stay in with her in my arms forever.

However, after they disappear, she says, "I should get some sleep, too."

"You're not going to sleep with me?"

She shakes her head. "I'll never get any if I stay with you. And we've got that three-hour drive before dawn if we're going to make my tee time."

My half-lidded gaze pops right open. "Three-hour drive? Where are we going?"

"Charleston. Where else?"

She's looking at me like I'm the crazy one.

"Why are we going to Charleston?" I persist.

"That's where the event is being held. It's at the Ocean Course on Kiawah Island. You know, where they played the Ryder Cup and the PGA Championship in the past. Didn't I tell you?"

"No," I say. "If I'd known that, I would have mentioned that's where my interview is, which makes everything a lot easier."

"Oh, sorry. With everything going, I must have forgotten to tell you."

She's forgotten to tell me many things. "What else do I need to know?"

"Nothing… Well, I got us hotel rooms?"

"Rooms?"

"Actually, a two-bedroom suite." She gives me a

sheepish look. "I didn't want to assume."

It feels like a step in the wrong direction. No way I'm going to go all clingy on her.

"Yeah, maybe you're right. How long will we be there?"

I didn't exactly pack for more than a few days. I thought I would have time to go home because I didn't want to bring a suitcase. I had a travel bag.

"Over a week—until the event is finished. Why?"

"I'm not sure I have enough clothes with me to wear. And if I drive home now, I won't be able to make the drive back. I could meet you there. I'll just leave from my place."

I watch as panic fills her expression. Then a light bulb calms her features.

"How about this? You won't let me pay you, so why don't you let me get you some clothes instead?"

I scrub a hand over my head. "No, thank you."

"What is it with you? Caddies don't work for free."

"Yeah, and I'm not a caddie. Plus, you're not getting paid for this event either. It's for charity. And besides, I've done well. I've made wise investment choices. I can afford to buy my own clothes."

"You're just stubborn and maybe a little sexist. I bet you're the type who thinks a woman shouldn't do anything for a man."

For a second I can't speak. "I may be a little old-fashioned, but I'm not a sexist. If anything, you've made my argument. Equal pay, right? You get paid zero, and so should I. If you were getting money, then I'd let you do something for me. Hell, I plan to pay for my own room."

"You will not." She points at me. "I swear, you will not pay for the room or any meals. And if you don't like it, stay here."

She marches off to her room, and I have to smile. It's that fierceness she has that really attracts me to her. I've dated beautiful women in all varieties, but this woman stirs my blood. And I like getting a rise out of her.

This trip should be fun with Riley in my bed. I'll also get the chance to meet with Rhoades. Who knows what could come of it. And maybe I'll end up finding a place to move to in Charlotte to start a new job and be closer to a certain fiery woman.

RILEY

This isn't the first time I've played the Ocean Course. It's tough, with the wind blowing in, but the views are spectacular, with the Atlantic, the marsh, and the gorgeous homes of the island. It's also wild and unstructured in most places on this end of the island, giving it a more uninhabited appearance.

"This is a dream come true," Mark says.

"I hope the kids see it that way. It's definitely a special place. Everybody always raves about Pebble Beach, and no doubt it's awesome, but there's just something about the Ocean Course that I love."

"Yeah, I can see why," Mark says. "Although I've never had the privilege of playing Pebble Beach."

"We'll have to do that sometime." I tee up the ball and take a swing. It flies straight down the middle of the fairway.

"Perfect shot," Mark says with an appreciative grin.

"Mark my distance."

"Got it. Is your coach here?"

"Yeah. He'll be around this week," I say. "What's my yardage?"

He holds up the tracker and announces proudly, "Two forty-eight. Damn, that's awesome."

The compliment slides right over me, my concentration too deep right now. The grip check Randy did on me seems to be holding. "Let's go." Mark grabs my club and puts it in my bag as I write down my yardage on the hole. We hop into the cart and drive to my ball. When we get to it, I remember something. "Hey, I showed you my ball mark, right?"

"No, you didn't."

"I do this on all my balls, even when I'm not playing in a tournament. Can you put a marker on the fairway for me?" When he places one where my ball is, I pick it up and show him. "See my three pink dots above the T in Titleist?"

"Yeah."

"Those are my marks, so I always know they're my balls," I explain.

"Yeah, that's a requirement, isn't it?" he asks.

"Yes, so nobody's balls get mixed up."

"Oh, yeah, I can see how that could be a big problem for someone if they get their balls mixed up," Mark says. His tone tells me all I need to know, and when I look at him, he can barely keep a straight face with his double entendre. I try so hard to act stern, but it's not possible to pull it off, and I end up letting a huge laugh rip out of me.

"Oh my God. Don't you dare do that to me during the event. I'll kill you."

He rubs his chin. "I'm sorry. I couldn't let that one go. The way you said it, you left the door wide open."

Shaking my head, I put my ball back on the fairway. "Okay, considering this is a par 5, which club should I use?" I'm testing him, and he knows it. He reads the yardage to the green and notices it's a dogleg to the left. Then he suggests a 3 wood.

"Why a 3 wood and not a 5?" I ask.

"You need the distance. Your driver will put you over, but your 5 won't get you close enough. Your 3 should get you within striking distance of the green, and hopefully you can birdie the hole."

"Read the hazards. What are they?"

He checks his information book on the hole and cringes. "My bad. I should've consulted this first. Use your 5."

I smile, saying, "That's why we're here for a week. Had I used a 3, I would've ended up ass over head in the bunker." I take the shot, and it's a nice one, putting me within striking distance. When we get close to the green, he sees the bunker I was referring to. There are three, and they are waist deep.

"Shit, if I had landed in there, I would've taken a mulligan."

"Yeah, well, mulligans aren't allowed in regulation,"

I say, nudging him with my elbow.

"Duh. I know that. But I would've had to take one anyway and wave the white flag."

He makes me chuckle. "You play a lot?" I ask.

"Not as much as I like, and you would certainly put me to shame."

"That's because it's my job. Like you would put me to shame in investing money. So, Caddie, which club?"

He checks my distance from the hole and advises me to use a 9 iron.

"You should probably ask how far I can hit with a 9 first."

"Hmm. Good idea," he says sheepishly.

"Hey, this is your first time out here. You're learning my game."

"Yeah, and you smack the shit out of a ball."

"How do you think I got in the LPGA?"

He takes off his cap and runs his hand through his hair. Then he crams his cap back on his head. Is this a sign of frustration? I hope not. I need to put him at ease. "You're doing a lot better than I thought you would."

"Wanna know something?" he asks.

"Sure."

"You intimidate me out here."

This is a complete surprise to me. "I do? Why?"

"Because I didn't expect you to be this awesome. I guess I knew you were good, but you're outstanding. Ryder told me once that if you had been born a male, you would've excelled in any sport you played because you have incredible hand-eye coordination. I can see that now."

"Thank you for the compliment, but you should know I'm driven and competitive. When I want something, I go after it. I started playing golf with my dad when I was a kid and fell in love with it. That was all it took. There were no other sports for me. And this is my job. You spend what, fifty hours a week working? I spend that much playing golf. Sometimes more."

"Sixty at least, but, Riley, it's more than that. You're gifted."

"Maybe, but I have to work hard, too."

"Yes, you do. So, how about we continue on here, Boss?"

"Okay, Caddie, back to my question about yardage with the 9 iron."

We debate which club, and I use the 9 to make a point. As I set up the shot, I look back at him and say, "Stop ogling my ass."

"I thought that came with the job." He waggles his brows at me. "Seriously, though, I'm checking out your stance. Something a good caddie would do."

"Sure you are." I take the shot, and it flies over the green.

"Holy fuck! Maybe a pitching wedge would've been better."

I crack up. "You think? But check my distance with that so you know."

"Damn, too bad the Yankees don't need a pinch

hitter. I bet you can knock the hell out of a baseball, too."

"I'm not too bad."

"Modesty," he mutters with mirth.

We drive around to the back of the green, and I chip my ball onto the green with a great shot, landing me inches from the hole.

"Jesus! Look at that shot!"

He's cracking me up. "Calm down, Caddie."

"You almost sunk that baby."

"That would've been a nice birdie hole if I had." As it is, I end up with a par. The rest of the day moves smoothly, with Mark picking up pointers and learning my game. By the end of our first round, he's acting a bit more comfortable.

"How about a stop at the nineteenth hole for some food?" I ask. The nineteenth hole is the place where golfers usually hang out after they play. It's not an actual hole, but a restaurant or bar at the golf club.

"Yeah, I'm starved." One of the course attendants comes up and asks if I want to check my clubs, but I tell him after we eat, we're heading to the range. Mark's eyes bulge out.

"The range? After eighteen holes?"

"Yeah. I need to hit a few hundred balls. Randy is supposed to meet us there this afternoon. Is that a problem?"

"Not at all. I only thought you'd be tired."

"Tired? This is nothing. We got a late start because

the course was wet, and now it gets dark earlier so I can't play as late. I usually play thirty-six holes and then go to the range and the putting green."

We order our food and eat when it arrives.

Mark is full of questions. "What about during the season?"

"Yeah, the travel is tedious. Living in hotels practically every week. Practice rounds and then the tournament. I pick and choose now, usually playing in the majors. But when I'm not in a tournament, I'm at home playing my ass off. And in the off-season is when I crank it up. I take a week off here and there, but it's not a lot of time. Golf isn't like the other sports where you have to rest your body. Unless you're injured, it's all-out."

"Do you work out?" he asks.

"I have a trainer. He works me hard three days a week. Forearms, shoulders, back, chest, legs, and core are what he concentrates on. And on the other days I run."

Leaning back in his chair, he stares with a furrowed brow. "Your life is brutal."

"I don't happen to think so. Sometimes I'm grumpy when I'm not hitting the ball like I want, but otherwise, I love what I do. It's the price you're willing to pay in order to do what you love is how I look at it. Professional athletes work their asses off. No one sees the behind the scenes of what we do."

"No, they don't. They only see the TV coverage." He

suddenly grabs my hand and says, "You have no idea how much respect I have for what you do."

Wow. I wasn't expecting this. It makes me warm and fuzzy, which is weird because not much does, especially where men are concerned.

"Thank you, Mark. That means a lot to me."

The check arrives and he moves to pay, but I stop him. "All your meals are covered, remember?"

Sitting back, he says, "Okay, but only for this event. And just for the record, I'm not a fan of this."

"Duly noted."

We leave and head to the range where I proceed to hit bucket after bucket of balls. Randy finally shows up, and I make the introductions. My coach isn't stupid. He scrutinizes Mark, and then me. His brain churns like an old-fashioned ice cream maker. Now he gets why I was so discombobulated the other day.

"So, Mark, how long have you known Riley?"

Before Mark can answer, I say, "A long time. Mark is my cousin, Fletcher's best friend."

"I see." And then Randy mumbles, "Hair twirling."

At the same time, I say, "Randy!" and Mark asks, "What?"

"Mark, don't pay any attention to him. He's going senile," I say.

Mark says, "He's not old enough for that. What aren't you telling me about this hair twirling?"

Randy says, "Her game was off the other day, and I accused her of hair twirling. Now I know why."

Since Mark's a finance guy, I see him doing some mental calculations. It doesn't take long for a satisfied grin to spread across his handsome face.

"See, I knew it," Randy yells. "Damn hair twirling."

I grab a different club out of my bag and stomp away from them. Mark looks like a male lion that just became king of the pride. But Randy, on the other hand, looks like the detective who uncovered the killer of JonBenét Ramsey, a murder that's been unsolved for twenty years. I only have one word for this—*men*.

But soon after, my pride soars, because as I'm hitting ball after ball, they're landing exactly where I'm aiming. Randy praises me, and Mark's eyes singe holes in my ass. There's no denying I'm in love with the fact that he can't seem to rip his gaze off of me. And I'm quickly laughing said ass off when Randy asks him, "Hey, aren't you supposed to be caddying for her?"

Mark says, "Yes, why?"

"You'd better start watching more of where her balls are landing instead of eyeing her butt much like an eager pup."

Mark, being the good sport he is, has nothing else to say, except, "Busted."

"You sure you're up for this? She's one of the top LPGA players." Randy is dead serious now.

"Yes, sir, I am. And I promise, no more butt ogling."

Randy is not buying it for a second, but Mark moves to my bag and starts busying himself with cleaning my club heads.

When the light begins to fade, Randy calls it a day. "Good job, Ri. When's your tee time tomorrow?"

"Ten," I say.

He looks at Mark when he answers, "See you then." He doesn't trust Mark at all to do the job. Tomorrow will be hilarious, with Randy ordering him around. I'll have to remind him that Mark is doing this out of kindness, and not because he is being paid.

When we get to our hotel, The Sanctuary, which is aptly named, Mark asks, "Is Randy always a caddie Nazi?"

I crack up. "He's protective and wants to make sure I do well. He also considers himself my second father, so watch yourself around him."

"No shit."

He shoves me into the room and says, "But for now, I've been teased by that ass of yours all fucking day, so it's only fair for you to bare it and share it now."

"Gladly." I pull off my jacket, shirt, and unzip my pants. When I'm down to my bra and panties, he stops me.

"Let me do that." He's a panty ripper. With his fingers on the elastic at my hips, he snaps it like it's nothing, and it falls to my feet in scraps.

"Those were Agent Provocateur. They cost a pretty penny."

"I'll replace them." His mouth covers mine as he unhooks my bra. Grabbing my ponytail, he spins me around and kisses my neck. And I mean *kisses my neck*.

Up and down, front and back, and each side until I'm a writhing mess in his arms. No other part of my body has been touched, only my neck, and I'm as wet as I've ever been.

He doesn't speak a word. All I know is I want him. *Now.* He strips, and I watch. Defined muscles point down to a sexy V and I go to touch, but he stops me. Instead, he reaches for my hands and puts them on one of the bedposts we're standing next to. It's a four-poster type, so I grab on to it and hear him tearing into a condom. His hands latch on to my hips and pull me out so I'm bent at the waist. Then his fingers reach between my thighs from behind and he slides one inside, I imagine to see how ready I am. And I am definitely ready. The finger is gone, but is replaced by his cock. He doesn't test the waters. He drives straight for the hole in one. And it's exactly what I needed.

"Hold on, baby. I'm taking you for a ride."

And does he ever. Each thrust lands balls deep with a slap, and he doesn't break stride at all. One hand holds me steady, while the other has playtime with my clit. I am on fire with heat and electricity, going from zero to eighty in no time flat. And when my orgasm detonates, it feels like the transformer on my electrical circuitry blew. If it weren't for his arm holding me up, I'd tumble to the floor.

Surprise, he's not done. He lays me flat on my stomach on the bed, with a pillow beneath my hips, and round two begins. The man is a machine. He does some rotational movement that I can't see, only feel, and it fires me up again. His mouth works on my neck again, and I'm squirming to the dance of his tongue. Deep moans come from my throat, and I couldn't prevent them if I wanted to.

But wait, he pulls out and flips me over, like a circus act. Then he lies next to me and rolls me to my side. When he's behind me, he slides back in and pulls my knees up. Hmm. This is great. It causes so much friction, I'm soon coming again. He bucks a few times, and I feel him coming, too.

Then it hits me. I may be in shape on the golf course, but I need to work out more in the bedroom. It strikes me as funny, so I laugh as he heads to the bathroom. When he returns from disposing the condom, he asks what's so comical and I fill him in.

"Guess we're going to change all that, aren't we?" he suggests.

"Yeah, I guess we are. Starting now."

"And do I have some plans for you."

"Plans? What kind of plans?" I ask.

"How adventurous do you like to get?"

"I'll try anything, except bondage and whips." The thought of being whipped freaks me out.

"No bondage at all? Not even the fun stuff?" he asks.

"Okay, maybe a little. But no whips and chains."

"I wouldn't do that, but I'd love to see you spread out on the bed, tied in silk," he says.

"Now that I could do."

"How about toys?" he asks.

"I love toys. I have some toys," I admit.

"We'll have to use them sometime. And … what about anal?"

"I'll try it. I've never done it, but I'm game."

He grabs me and kisses me. "I think this will be a lot of fun."

"Just remember, we have Randy to deal with. I have to get sleep. And our adventures in bed can't affect my game."

"No, never," he promises.

Tomorrow will tell. And if they ever do, he'll have to deal with Randy, too.

MARK

Riley goes to sleep, but I go to work. I might not have a job with a firm, but I work for myself. I play catch-up with the financial news of the day and make decisions about the directions of my investments for tomorrow. I read through emails and find that I've received a few from previous clients at my former job. The common theme between them is they want to find out where I landed.

I carefully craft responses that I haven't accepted any job opportunities at the moment, but may have an answer soon. Any position I accept will come with the expectation that I will bring new clients with me.

It's a little after one in the morning when I finally crawl into my bed, alone. I could have gotten in bed with her, but I didn't want to wake her. Plus, I'm certain I wouldn't be able to keep my hands to myself.

My eyes have barely closed when an alarm blares in my ear. I open my lids to see a playful Riley hovering over me with her phone held near my ear. Groaning, I roll over.

"Come on, Wall Street. You have ten minutes before we have to get out of here. I ordered breakfast."

Tired as shit, I roll out of bed and take the fastest shower known to man. I barely have a chance to take two bites of eggs before Riley is shoving me out the door. I'm sleepy and grumpy, but manage to keep a smile plastered to my face as Randy gives me shit the whole day for not keeping eagle eyes on Riley.

We've been at it for nearly six hours when Randy and Riley talk to themselves off to the side. He's giving her crap about her posture before, during, and after her swing. I let my eyes drift shut for one second before he's launching into me.

"If you're not taking this seriously, maybe I should caddie for Riley this week."

I close my mouth. Many thoughts want to burst from my mouth. I almost say *you act more like you want to be her husband than her coach or a second father*. Somehow, I manage to keep it to myself.

"Randy, stop. He's obviously tired."

"Then he's not up to the challenge."

Riley starts to say something else, but fed up, I beat her to it. "You know, he might be your better option. Last thing I want to do is ruin your game."

I'm not a quitter, but I've had enough. Quite possibly if I'd had more sleep, I could have taken all the jabs he's thrown at me all day. But right now, I want to slug the guy. Better to walk away than have Riley think me a violent man.

"Mark, wait," Riley calls.

I don't look back, because if I see her face, I'll surely cave. And it's in our best interest I leave now. So I lift a hand and wave goodbye.

Following the cart path, I head back to the clubhouse and call the hotel for a ride back to The Sanctuary. Once there, before I can sleep, I read through the *Wall Street Journal* and *Investor's Business Daily*. I check the trends for the day and make adjustments in my investment portfolio.

Next, I check my email inbox, and I have a reply from one of the clients I responded to yesterday. I end up reading through his email twice. He wants me to continue working on his portfolio personally until I find another firm. His words, he doesn't want to chance his money with anyone else. I grin to myself.

Throughout the years, I've toyed with the idea of going at it on my own. However, the overhead and risk had been too high for me then. I'm no longer a rookie at this with lofty dreams. Now a seasoned guy, it's something to consider.

I send a quick reply to the guy that we should talk and come up with terms. It's not as easy as me running his accounts on the side. It needs to be legal, so I can't be sued for hacking into his account and doing crazy things he doesn't agree to. I'll have to contact a lawyer to draw up a contract.

Just as I'm about to send an email to Ben Rhoades to tell him I'm in town, Riley comes through the door. I can't tell if she's pissed at me or at the world until she stops in front of me.

"What the hell, Mark? Do you always leave when things get tough?"

She has a right to her opinion since I didn't complain that I hadn't had enough sleep the last few nights between working and making love to her. I also don't want to fight over something stupid like words said out of foolish anger.

"Randy's right. I'm not the right choice for you."

Holding her gaze, she chews on her lower lip, and I see some of the fight leave her. "I'm sorry," she says quietly. "Randy was out of line."

"He's got your best interest at heart." As much as I hate the guy at the moment, that much I believe.

"Still, he had no right to beat up on you all day. He's worried I'll be distracted like I was the last time I dated someone."

A part of me wonders whom she dated that fucked up her game, and if she still cares for that guy.

"We're dating?" I say instead, playing it off as a joke.

"What do you call it? I'm not in the business of sleeping around. I'm not saying we're on the path to marriage or anything, but I assume we're at least exclusive."

I haven't really thought about it. However, I don't like the idea of her being with someone else.

"Yeah, okay."

Steadfast in the point she wants to make, she ignores my comment.

"Well, he sees you as an obstacle, a disruption to my game."

Scooting the chair back, I pull her down onto my lap because my need to touch her when she's near overcomes me.

"I get that you're competitive and he wants you to be the best, but this is a charity event. He acts like this will somehow affect your golf ranking. And as much as I want to help you and be there for you to win like the winner you are, I'm not up to being chastised like a child for the next week to come."

She squirms on my lap, because while I spoke, I worked my hand under her shirt to cup her breast.

"Believe me, I talked to him. He was under the impression that I was paying you, and therefore at his mercy as much as mine. I told him you refused payment, and to be honest, I think that made him respect you more."

"Honestly, I don't care what he thinks of me. I care about you. And if I stayed there any longer, I might have taken our argument in a different direction."

I pinch her nipple, and she arches her back against me. "So you'd hit an old man."

She takes my other hand and puts it between her legs.

"I didn't want to, which is why I walked away."

Taking my fingers, she strokes them over her clit.

"So you're the bigger man."

"Flattery will get you everywhere," I joke.

"I would laugh if I didn't need you right now." She places a kiss on my lips. "Did I ever tell you I don't have any gag reflex?"

If my dick hadn't already been hard since she strode through the door, it would have gotten there now. She slides off my lap, never letting her eyes drift from mine. When she unzips my pants, junior pops out like a jack-in-a-box. I raise my hips, letting her tug my shorts down. My dick bobs until she circles her hand around it.

When she takes me in her mouth, my muscles tighten in anticipation. The warmth of her makes my heart race, and all I want to do is bend her over the desk and fuck the shit out of her.

On her knees, she shows me that she can manage to swallow me whole. It's sexy as fuck. I cup the sides of her head and guide her up and down my length. She hollows her cheeks, forcing me closer to the edge. Pulling her free, I take her by the shoulders and spin her around.

"I hate that we have to use a condom," I mutter.

"Me, too," she says as I bend down to get my shorts and come up with a foil packet.

"Always prepared, even if we are on the green."

"A guy can hope," I say, tearing the foil.

I don't mention that I have every intention of fucking her on the course, one way or another. Quickly, I roll it on and seat her fully on me. But the furniture in front of us calls to me.

"Grab the desk."

She does, and we lose the chair. I love watching her ass, but as I slide in and out, I need that connection between us. I pull out and turn her around. Then I press her back against the surface. I lift her legs at the knees and slide back in. I groan, louder than the sounds of her sweet moans. Her breasts bounce with our movement between us, so I lean over and suck one into my mouth. She bucks, wanting her clit to be stroked. I maneuver my hand between us to do just that. Then I take her mouth, stroking her tongue the same way I stroke between her legs until she's vibrating around my dick. It doesn't take long before I follow her into oblivion.

We stay like that, panting for long minutes, until I kiss her one last time before helping her to her feet.

"I'm going to take a shower," she offers. "Join me."

"Give me a minute. I need to send out this email to Rhoades first."

"Are you really considering moving here to South Carolina to work?"

"The interview is here, but the opportunity is to open a satellite office in Charlotte. You can't get rid of me yet."

"Oh." She looks relieved.

I want to, but I don't read anything into that yet. What we have is new. And what I've learned over the years is we're in the honeymoon phase of whatever is between us.

"But the good thing is, after I send this email, I'm all yours. I've taken care of everything else for the day."

She frowns. "You're still working."

I laugh. "I have to keep current with the trends and take care of my portfolio along with my families'. If I don't keep up with what's going on, I won't be good for anyone to hire me."

"Wow, I guess I didn't think about it. Is that why you were so tired today?"

"You noticed?" Though she'd said it to Randy, I hadn't been sure if she was making excuses for me, or if she knew the truth.

She nods. "I caught you yawning a few times. I thought maybe it was me."

I stand and circle my arms around her waist.

"I'd gladly lose sleep for you."

"Really."

"Yeah, I'll follow your lead, just how I let you kiss me that summer."

Incredulous, she narrows her eyes at me. "That's not how I remember it. You were practically begging me to let you kiss me."

"Begging, huh?"

"Absolutely, on your hands and knees and everything." She laughs.

"Truthfully," I begin. "I kicked myself for days after you left wondering why in the hell I waited so long."

"Why did you?"

Pushing a hand through my hair, I answer honestly.

"Hell, I was sure you'd slap me when I told you."

"Slap you? I wanted to ask you what took you so long, and I might have if Ryder hadn't have shown up."

I go in for the kiss, remembering that first time. There is an insatiable need in me every time I'm with her. So I pull back, otherwise we'll never get any sleep tonight.

"Go ahead and start the shower. I'll only be a few minutes."

I tap her sweet ass before she walks naked toward her bathroom, stirring my dick to life again. *Down, boy.* I need to write a professional email to Rhoades. Last thing I need to do is slip up and write some stupid shit because there's not enough blood flowing to my brain. I think about the bear market we're in right now, and that's enough to have my dick softening. Then I compose my email. However, when I close my laptop, I hear the water running in the shower. That's enough to make me picture a wet Riley waiting for me. And I practically jog to the bathroom, determined not to miss a second more of that.

RILEY

It's ten o'clock when we show up at the course. Randy isn't there, so Mark and I do the usual of heading to the first tee. Things are more relaxed when my coach isn't around. But it doesn't last long. He meets us after the ninth hole, where we grab a quick bite to eat.

"So, investments, huh?" Randy asks. He is totally checking Mark out, and it's pissing me off. It's not like we're getting married or anything.

"Yes, sir." Mark isn't giving him much, and I want to laugh. There is definite head-butt potential here.

Randy then asks Mark, "So, how's she hitting 'em today?"

"I would think that's a question you'd be asking her."

Randy squares his shoulders and says, "Normally I would, but I want to see if you're up to par."

"Again, you should check with her on that."

Time to run interference. "Okay, gents, let's take it

down a notch. Randy, lay off. I'm hitting them damn good, actually. Mark is doing a great job, too. If you want answers, ask me. I'm a big girl, you know."

Mark wears a self-satisfied grin. He needs a little admonishing, too. "And, Mark, you have to understand Randy's position. He wants me to be number one, so cut the old man a little slack."

"Old man?" Randy practically screams.

"Come on. You know I'm just playing with you. But you are being antagonistic, so stop."

Randy wears a sheepish expression, so he's gotten my point.

"You two only have to get along until Sunday. And then you can hate each other all you want. But I need you to accommodate each other, for my sake, until this event is over. Can you do that for me? Please?" I flutter my eyes at both of them, and they chuckle.

"Yes," they both say. Then I wonder how Randy will act if I ever do decide to get married. I'm sure the lucky guy will have to walk over hot coals or broken glass with bare feet. Or even sleep on a bed of nails.

My back nine is even better than the front, and Randy can't stop complimenting me. "If you play this well, you might beat some of the men."

"I'd like to think that. It means more money for the kids," I say.

Mark and I get into our cart and Randy follows in his to the driving range. I don't hit as many balls there as usual, but instead, head to the putting green. On the way, Mark asks if it would be much of a problem for me if he goes back to the room.

"I emailed Ben Rhoades earlier, and he wants to get together while I'm down here for that interview. Since Randy's here, I was wondering if you'd mind too much."

When I don't immediately answer, he jumps in and says, "It's okay. I don't have to go."

"Of course, you have to go. But I also need you to know how to help me read the greens. That's one of my biggest failures as a golfer."

"Then I'll stay," he says, grabbing my hand. "I don't want to let you down."

"But this is a charity event. You need to go. It's your livelihood."

"I'll email him from here and tell him I'll have to do it in the evening, that's all."

"Why don't you do this? Hit the putting green with me for a little while and then head back. Make your plans and do what you have to. I'll be fine."

He hesitates, and I say, "Do it. This is an opportunity you should check out."

"Okay, I will."

While I'm practicing my putting, Randy gives Mark a few pointers before Mark leaves. Then I wrap up the day, and we head to the clubhouse.

"How about a beer?" he asks.

"Sure."

We're seated at the bar, enjoying the view when I hear, "Riley, I was glad to see your name on the roster."

The voice sends a wave of anxiety laced with anger ripping through me. It's the same voice that made all kinds of wonderful promises to me, and the one I heard moaning out some other woman's name when I walked into his house for a surprise visit. I haven't seen him since that night—the night he pretty much made me look like the biggest fool in the world.

"I bet you were, Justin."

"You're looking good." Then he notices Randy sitting next to me. He dips his head and says, "Hi, Randy. Hope you're well."

"Better than you are, I'm sure."

Randy says that because ever since we broke up, Justin's career took a nosedive, while mine soared.

"So, you here alone?" he asks.

I can't believe the douche wants to know that.

"No. I brought my entourage." Sarcasm weighs down my tone.

"Your—" It sinks in, and he chuckles. The thing that kills me is that man is still hot. I wonder if he's still fucking every woman he can get his fingers in and on.

I reach for my beer, looking away, hoping he'll leave. No luck there.

"So, Riley, congratulations on your amazing year. You really knocked it out."

"Thanks," I say, not the type to be a bitchface.

Damn, if the man doesn't order a beer and pull up a seat next to me. Randy kicks my leg.

"So yeah, the Wilde twins dominated the sports

news this year. Your brother rocked it, too, didn't he?"

"Sure did." I hope my brief responses will clue him in. But no. As usual, the dumbass keeps yapping away.

"The World Series. Holy shit. How cool was that?"

"Very."

Randy is about to burst out laughing, and I have to flash him the stink eye, so he averts his gaze to the huge window and doesn't even dare glance my way.

Then the fidiot asks, "Did you get one of those cancer kids to play with you?"

My fuse has reached the stick of dynamite it's attached to, and I blow. "Justin, what in the actual fuck do you think we are all here for? Every golfer is assigned *one of those cancer kids to play with*, you moron. It's a fundraiser for the Make-A-Wish Foundation. And each of those children has requested a certain golfer they want to play with. Why any of them chose you, I have no idea."

"Jeez, Riley, that's a bit harsh, isn't it?"

"No, Justin, what's harsh is that you don't have a clue what's going on here. And what's even harsher is that those poor kids are dying, and one of their last wishes on Earth is to play golf with us. It's an *honor*, Justin. Treat it as one."

"Yeah. Sorry. I didn't think—"

"See, that's your problem. You don't think." I guzzle the rest of my beer because it's time for me to get the hell out of here. I can't be around this guy.

"Randy, I'm headed back. You ready?"

He jumps out of his seat, and we leave. When we get outside, to where the transportation stand is, he says, "Damn, Riley, you bit that poor guy's head off."

I cringe, saying, "I know, but his stupidity grated on me to the point where I exploded."

"Do you think it was a little more than that?"

"What do you mean?"

The hotel van arrives, and we get in. Then Randy says, "Maybe you've been holding that anger in for all this time."

He has a valid point because I have. When it all went down, Justin saw me standing in the doorway. I ran out of there and he followed, saying the usual stuff—she's nothing, I don't love her, blah, blah, blah. But it was over, and I broke it off. Only I never let him have it. I was hurt at first, but the anger came later. Today was the manifestation of that.

"You're right. But he deserved it, especially after the comment he made about those poor kids."

"True, and you should've seen his face. Was he always that dimwitted?"

"I guess so. Maybe I was blinded by his beauty." And we're both silent for a couple of seconds, right before I burst out laughing.

"Riley, you could've handled it a bit better. He looked like he got hit in the head with a hammer."

"He did. The Wilde Hammer!"

I chuckle the rest of the way back to the hotel, which is only about five more minutes. Randy doesn't appreciate the humor, but I don't care. I'm still chuckling when I get to my room, and Mark wants to know what's so funny. Not wanting to get into the whole Justin story, I divert his attention by asking about his interview.

His arm curls around my waist, and he says, "I actually have a breakfast meeting with him." My heart falls. "But don't worry. He's meeting me out here at seven thirty. I told him what I'm doing, so he gets why my schedule is so cramped. I explained how I'd have to be finished by nine thirty. He's promised we would. So I'm all yours afterward."

Relief makes me smile in return. "That's perfect. For a minute there you gave me a scare."

"Hey, I'm all in for this. If I have to leave you, it'll only be for an hour or whatever. But I've got your back, Eagle. Don't forget that."

Justin said that to me once, and the only thing he had of mine was my pussy. He didn't care about anything else. I wonder if Mark is trustworthy. Gina said he was, but they're friends. Well, except for high school and that doesn't count.

"What's wrong? Something's bothering you. I can tell."

"No, I'm fine. Really." Shaking off thoughts of my old boyfriend, I put my arms around Mark's neck and say, "So, what're our plans for tonight?"

"I thought we could do dinner here if that's okay?"

"Absolutely, as long as it's not late. You have an early wake-up call."

"You read my mind."

Then something dirty comes to mind. "Can I ask a favor of you?"

"Anything."

I walk up to him and unzip his pants. "Anything?"

"Hmm-mmm."

"Good." When his pants are off and his boxers pushed down, he stands there, fully erect. I take his cock and feel the smooth yet steely length in my fist. I pump him a few times, then I say, "I want to watch you get yourself off."

His gaze burns into me before he says, "Strip and get on the bed." Pulling up the desk chair, he faces the end of the bed, where I sit. He removes the rest of his clothes and takes a seat. Then he stares, but the man looks so good, I'm not sure this was such a great idea. Now I want to sink my fingers into his flesh and have him fuck me until I scream. But I don't move a muscle. I don't even blink.

"Is this what you want?"

He fists his cock and slides his hand up and down so slowly, I moan, "Yes."

"And this?" He repeats his action again. And again. Until he picks up a little speed. His cock is hard, and all I want to do now is wrap my lips around it and suck it off. But I'm locked in my position on the bed, trapped by the scene before me. My hand moves between my thighs and runs up and down my slit.

"Open up your sweet pussy for me. I want to see all

of you." Using one hand to spread my lips, I use the other to rub my clit.

"Use your fingers inside you," he orders. "Two."

His movement has picked up, and one hand is now on the arm of the chair, gripping it tightly. I'm drenched. I feel it pooling around my hand.

"You're so wet. I can see it from here. Do you like to see me get myself off?"

"Yes," I hiss. And I do. It's fucking sexy as hell, watching him grip his own cock.

"Make yourself come, Riley. I want to see how you do it. What you like."

I use one finger to rub my clit in a circular motion. But I think what gets me off the most is the visual of him holding his dick. It's a gorgeous cock—large, tanned with a pinkish hue—and currently the head is slick with his pre-ejaculate. As those thoughts careen through my brain, I come, panting his name. And then I watch him erupt, shooting streams of cum, and it spurs me to action. I fly off the bed, and wrap my hand over his, helping to give him his happy ending. When he's done, I rub his cum all over his cock, playing with the stuff. Too bad he wears a condom when we have sex.

Our mouths crash together in a storm of need, and too soon, he says, "I need to clean up before we do anything."

"A shower?" I suggest.

"Good idea. Don't forget a condom."

"On it."

I get the water ready and wait for him. My body's ready for round two. I hope my heart and brain are because he's already getting me twisted up.

MARK

The next night, unable to sleep, I roll out of bed and stretch. Riley's naked body is tempting. However, it would be unfair for me to wake her up for round three when she's got to be her best on the green tomorrow. Besides, there is plenty I can do. I grab a pair of gym shorts and put them on before heading to my computer to do some work.

The laptop lies open, untouched, as I think about my meeting earlier with Ben and Martin from Rhoades Investments. Ben had taken care of much of the interview. By the time it was over, he said to me, "I'm just going to be honest and say we've had our eye on you for a while. Talented finance people who don't work for the big New York guys are hard to come by."

He'd ended up offering between salary, incentives, benefits, and perks nearly twice what I'd received at my former job. It should be a no-brainer.

But I've gotten several more emails and a few calls

from more of my former clients. Most of them are willing to go with me, no matter where I end up. So, what if I go it alone?

The idea of freedom to do things the way I see fit intrigues the hell out of me. I can buy a house in Asheville or even move back to Waynesville with a designated office area and set up shop. There's something about being my own boss that's appealing. Setting my hours and being able to get up after making love to a beautiful woman like now to do work is looking better and better. Granted, I'll have to spend more time watching the market during business hours than I've been able to do. Still...

However, working for Rhoades, I will essentially run the Charlotte office with no one to answer to other than Ben and his father, Martin. And as long as everything runs smoothly, we would only have weekly videoconference meetings, or so he claims.

Riley walks out of the room, rubbing her arms. "I'm cold," she pouts.

"Being naked can do that," I tease.

Seeing her standing there instantly gives me wood. And the temptress heads straight for me. The idea of getting anything done has me closing my laptop and pushing it to the side. I give her a place to sit by letting her stand between my legs with her ass brushing the desk.

"I'm cold because you left me alone, and I missed you."

"Hmm, sounds like I have some making up to do."

She nods and scoots to sit on the desk just as I planned. I roll my chair forward, spreading her legs in the process. Her pussy is gorgeous, smooth, and wide open to me.

"A midnight snack sounds good," I murmur.

I press my hand to her chest, pushing her back some and dipping my head to lick her sweet sex.

It isn't long before Riley pants, "You and your talented tongue."

Sucking in her clit earns me an immediate response from her. She fists my hair and jams my face between her legs. Working with her need, I thrust my tongue into her pretty cunt and fuck her with it until I get my fingers in position. Switching gears, I slide two fingers into her and free up my mouth to kiss the lips between her legs, tonguing them and circling her swollen nub. I curl my fingers inside to touch that button that will send her shooting off like a bottle rocket. Her walls start to contract, and she tightens her grip on my hair. She doesn't let go until she's crested the wave. I have to fist my dick so I don't shoot off. She's so extraordinarily stunning when she comes.

Riley isn't selfish. She sees my problem and removes my hand. There is nothing fucking sexier than watching a woman go down on you. As much as I love being inside her, I will not last staring at her beautiful lips wrapped around my cock and sucking it down her throat. I try to hold out because it feels fucking amazing as I jackhammer into her mouth. When I come, it's hard. My legs lock, and I have a death grip on her head.

"Fuck," I groan, finally coming back to myself.

She sucks at the head, sending unbearable tingles through my body. And she knows she's a fucking pro, teasing me with a self-satisfying smirk on her face.

I cup the back of her head and draw her up for a kiss. She tastes like me, and I like it. It fucking turns me on again. I stand and wrap her legs around me to carry her back to bed. Tomorrow, she's going to be tired, and Randy's going to be pissed. But he'll have to deal because I can't get enough of this woman.

When the alarm goes off in the morning, Riley isn't a happy camper while she heads for the shower. Guilty for keeping her up, I throw on some clothes to grab us something quick to eat from the coffee shop downstairs. There's no time this morning for room service.

On the other side of the door, a man in a golf shirt holds a bag and a tray with two coffees. He looks familiar, but I'm wondering why he's here as he dons the same confused expression I'm wearing.

"Can I help you?"

"Actually, I'm looking for Riley Wilde. Maybe the concierge gave me the wrong room number."

My first thought is to give the hotel staff shit for giving out private information. Then I check myself. I don't know who this guy is to Riley. He might have every right to know what room she's in.

"No, you have the right room. She's in the shower

right now."

"Oh, okay. I'll wait."

He eyes the keycard I'm holding. What can I say? No, you can't go in. Again, I want to so badly. However, this could all be a misunderstanding on my part.

"Why don't I go tell her you're waiting?"

Using my key, I open the suite, and he follows me inside like he owns the place. I turn around to tell him to wait here, and his hand is extended.

"I'm Justin Turner, by the way. And you are?"

Shaking his hand, I recognize his name and now his face. He used to be the number three golfer in the world. In the past, I admired his game. *Not anymore*, I think. Especially if he and Riley have a history.

"Mark," I say, trying to keep jealousy at bay.

"Mark. Are you her assistant?"

So many things I can say, none of them quite adequate. Riley and I have agreed on exclusivity when it comes to sex, but we haven't labeled anything else we are.

"I'm caddying for her."

His brows lift in relief. "Oh, I've never seen you before. Have you caddied for anyone else I might know?"

"Not exactly." This isn't my world, and somehow I'm sure explaining what I'm doing will only make him think less of me than he already does. Besides, it's up to Riley to tell this guy what she wants him to know. "She has an early tee time, so let me go tell her you're here."

Before I say something wrong, I stride away. Riley's

not mine, I chant in my head.

I close the bedroom door and hear the shower cut off. When I step inside the bathroom, she stares at me funny, and I know I need to check my ego before I speak.

"Hey, that was quick," she says, looking fucking edible as slick and wet.

"Actually, someone is here to see you. He brought breakfast for the two of you. I'll go grab something downstairs and give you two a chance to *talk*."

I don't mean to say the word that way. So I flash her a smile and hope I don't resemble the clown from Stephen King's movie, *It*.

"Mark," she calls, as I try to leave and not say anything that would make me look like a dick.

"Yeah." I don't break stride.

The doorknob is in my hand when she says, "Who's out there?"

"His name is Justin."

Then I move. I'm out both doors and pressing the button several times for the elevator. The devil on my right shoulder is shouting at me for being a dumbass and leaving. Should I have stayed and marked her as mine? If they have a history, will he go into the room and catch her naked?

Trust is hard when you've been burned like I have. But I do trust her, even though all I have is her body. And I recognize what I'm feeling. Jealousy is bred from one thing. And I realize I want more than sex from this woman. I want her heart.

RILEY

What the hell? Why did Mark tear out of here like his hair was on fire, and what in the world is Justin doing here? And why would Mark let him in and leave me here alone? A pit of anger develops in my gut, but quickly expands into the equivalent of a nuclear explosion. Stomping in the room, I rip open drawers, pull out clothes, and get dressed. Then I practically tear all my hair out by the roots when I yank my brush through it. Why do men have to be so damn stupid? Muttering a slew of curse words, beginning with *shit* and ending with *fuck*, I sling the door of my bedroom open, startling Justin when I nearly rip the heavy thing off the hinges.

"What the hell did you say to Mark?"

"Huh," a shocked Justin says.

"Mark. My boyfriend. What did you say to him?"

"Your boyfriend?"

Tilting my head to the ceiling, I pray for patience so I

don't strangle the motherfucker. "Yes, the guy who let you in here. My boyfriend, Mark."

"He said he was your caddie."

"He is my caddie for this event, but he's also my boyfriend. And how did you get my room number?"

Justin fishmouths a few times, and then admits, "I told the concierge I was your fiancé."

"You did what?" I screech.

He finally gets to his feet and shifts from one foot to the other. "Uh, yeah. I knew they wouldn't just randomly give out your room number, so I sort of fibbed."

Now it's my turn to play guppy. I am so furious, I can't even speak. My voice has fled the island. The man fucking lied! When I can pull enough oxygen into my starved lungs to allow me to formulate a coherent sentence, I say to him in a low voice, "I'm going to tell you this one time. Get. Out. Of. This. Room. If you ever do anything like this again, I will cut your penis off."

"But, Riley, I was hoping—"

"Did you hear what I said? Get out now. Or I'm calling security."

He actually takes the time to gather up the breakfast he brought and leaves. Now I have to figure out where the hell Mark is. I call his cell phone, but as I suspect, he doesn't answer. So I text him where to meet me. Checking the time, I see I only have about thirty minutes until my tee time. I'll be surprised if I don't hit the ball all the way to Africa today. And to top it off, if this can even be topped, I don't have time to eat, and the dumb fuck who ruined it all took his breakfast with him. Motherfuckingasshole!

When I get to the clubhouse, I grab a gigantic cup of coffee, a protein bar, and head to the carts, where my clubs await me. Mark stands there, sheepishly, and when I see him, I want to scream. But I don't. I bite my tongue and get behind the wheel of the cart.

When he gets in, he makes the mistake of asking, "Did you have a nice chat?"

"What did he tell you? Justin, I mean. You flew out of there so fast."

By this time, we're at the number one tee box. I dig through the pocket of my bag, pull out a tee, set up my ball, and tee off without even taking aim. Everything I did was wrong, and I end up hooking the ball. It flies left off the fairway and into the rough. It's bad. Really bad. I can't help but feel how much my life resembles that ball right now. The rough on the course is knee deep. I'd rather be an inch deep in the bunker. A stream of unladylike words flies out of my mouth.

"Um, that wasn't your best," Mark says.

I wish I could wake up and start the day over again, sans Justin. "Why did you let him in? He lied to the concierge to get my room number."

"What?"

"Justin. Why did you let him in? Are we not exclusive?"

"Yes, of course, we are."

"So, some guy who you never met, shows up at our

hotel door, and you let him in. I just want you to know that I'll never let some strange woman into our room. What I consider exclusive and what you do must be two different things."

He certainly wears confusion well, I'll give him that. "It wasn't like that. I figured he was a friend of yours. When I told you his name, you never said you didn't know him."

"I know him, but he's no friend. Justin and I dated in the past, but I caught him cheating on me and dropped him like a hot poker. And do you know what? It was the best thing that ever happened because the guy's a moron. And it freed me up for you."

Mark stares at me with a possessive expression, and the corners of his mouth curve upward.

But we can't stand here and debate this issue. Instead of doing that, I tee up another ball, which is totally against regulation, but at this point, I don't give a fuck. I'll deal with it later. This time I hit a perfect shot. We don't say much during the front nine. When we make the turn, he offers to grab me some food, and I gladly take him up on it. I use the restroom, and when we get back, we're off to the back nine. I'm glad Randy's not around. While I'm playing fairly well, considering, my mood is shit.

We're approaching number seventeen when Mark says, "I'm sorry."

The rest of the game is played in silence, and I'm glad for the concentration it affords me. Afterward, I head to the pitching green. My drives have been consistent, other than the first one, so I'm going to concentrate on pitching and hitting some shots out of the sand trap. After a couple of hours, I call it a day. We head back together, and I go straight to the hotel bar for a drink. Mark follows. When I move to sit at the bar, he steers me in a different direction. We end up sitting at a private booth, back in the corner. After our drinks are delivered and we take a few sips, he begins.

"I realized something today." He paused. "Do you want to know what?"

"What?"

He still holds my hand when he says, "I want you to be mine. As in my girl. And only my girl."

I draw circles on the table with the index finger of my other hand. "See, this is where the confusion comes in. I thought I already *was* your girl. And I have to admit that the fact that we've said we're exclusive, and spending this kind of time together you still had some doubts, really blows." The truth is, it's more than confusion. It hurts. It hurts that he didn't feel the same.

"You *are* my girl. At least I think of you that way."

"Then let's start fresh and put this behind us."

"And how do you propose we do that?" he asks, with a devilish look in his eye.

"Just wait until we get back to the room. I'm totally going to show you."

And I do. We barely make it inside the door, where I pull his pants down to his knees and start sucking him off. I've pushed him against the wall, and have him deep in my throat. One hand massages his sack while the other fists the base of his cock. His heavy breathing spurs me one. My cell phone beeps, but I ignore it, continuing to work his cock over. Releasing him for a second, an impish smile creeps over my face. I lick my finger and he moans, but my mouth covers his cock again. My wet finger slides inside his puckered hole, and he lets out a long, deep groan. I can almost count the seconds before his cum shoots down my throat as I suck him dry.

My phone beeps again, but now I'm ready for some action. Mark's eyes are heavy and sex-filled. His lips entice me to my feet because I want to kiss him, and he fills my mouth with his eager tongue. My shirt lands at my feet, along with my bra. He takes a nipple into his mouth and draws on it, pulling and biting. When he releases me, he says, "I had no idea you liked to play so dirty, Riley." My pants follow the rest of my clothing to the floor. He fumbles around a minute, which I assume he's searching for a condom.

"I'm going to fuck you till you scream." Then he pulls me to the couch and has me lie, stomach down, over the arm on the end. He enters from behind, slowly, and then pulls all the way out. "Knees together," he instructs. When he slides in and out again, he says, "Lock your ankles." And, oh, it's so good. The tightness, the friction is crazy. Every time he pushes inside, my pelvis hits the arm, and the pressure on my clit sends me closer to the edge. "Is this good?" he asks.

"Yes," I moan my answer.

"Good. You'll like this even better." Then he lets out a deep chuckle as he plays tit for tat. He's copying me. Hands spread my cheeks, and his finger rims my back door. With a little nudge, he pushes his way in.

The sensations are triple-timing me. Between the sofa arm, his dick, and finger, I'm coming all over the place. One of his hands grips my hip, and he lets out his release, too.

Suddenly, there's a loud bang on the door. "Riley, you in there?"

Shit, it's Randy.

Turning, I look at Mark and cover my lips, telling him to keep quiet.

"Riley, open the door, or I'm letting myself in."

The fuck. He has a key. I always give him one, dammit.

"Hang on a minute," I yell.

"You're late for your photo shoot with the kids. They've been waiting on you. Get your ass down there."

"Shit."

Mark pulls out, we jump up, and I run to the bathroom, trying to get myself in order.

"Riley, come on," Randy yells. "What the hell are you doing?"

Mark runs in the room, half-dressed. "What should I do?"

"Get dressed and get out there. Tell him I had a headache or ate something that upset my stomach."

"Which one?" he asks.

"Yeah." I'm so flustered I can't think straight.

"I'll tell him something upset your stomach."

"Yeah." Fuck. I race to get dressed when he leaves. I hear the door open and Randy's voice. It's raised, but then Mark tells him and he calms down somewhat.

"Why didn't she call me?"

"Guess she forgot."

When I join them, I feel like I just ran a marathon.

"You okay?" Randy asks.

"Yeah, better. Sorry I didn't call." Boy, do I feel guilty as hell.

As we head to the door, Randy puts on the brakes, bends down, and holds something between his thumb and index finger. "Stomachache, huh?"

Mark and I look at what he's holding, and it's an empty condom wrapper. Shit.

"And is that why your clothes are over there?"

Double-decker shit. With whipped cream on top.

MARK

Riley's beautiful, but she's so much more so as she poses for pictures with the Make-A-Wish kids. And there's nothing fake about her radiant smile or the quiet conversations she has with each of them. She doesn't speak loud to be heard or to have the reporters gathered there to collect sound bites, unlike Justin. I've lost all respect for him as he continues to say ridiculous one-liners to the kids that can be overheard by the crowd.

"She's great, isn't she?"

I look down at Randy, whom I had the unfortunate pleasure of standing next to the entire time. His glower has been constant when aimed in my direction. I've done my best to ignore it.

"There is a reason she's America's darling," I muse.

"And you're going to mess that all up."

I've been biting my tongue, but now I turn to face him. "Why don't you say what you really want to,

Randy?"

He doesn't waste time. "Okay, here it is. You're bad business for Riley. This coming year she has a shot at number one. She's playing the best I've seen her play. She doesn't have time for distractions. Honestly, she's better off hooking up occasionally with Justin when she needs someone. He gets it. He gets her. And he's busy himself, unlike you. He won't be an attention-needing man. You don't have a job. Therefore, you're demanding more of her time than she really has to give."

I'm about to lay into him, when Riley's hand lands on my arm. "Hey, you two. Sorry it took so long."

For her, I lose my glower. "You looked great up there." I lean in and kiss her lips. Yes, I want to do that, but I also want Randy to see that he's not going to push me away. "You are so fucking awesome."

She grins and hikes herself up to whisper something back. "You're fucking awesome, too, on the green, in my bed, against the wall, between my legs."

I lower my hand to slide down her back and pat her butt. "Stop, you're getting my dick hard. You're going to have to stand in front of me the rest of the time if you keep at it."

Spinning around, she presses her back to my chest and wiggles her ass against me.

"You're not playing fair," I say, nuzzling in her hair to speak in her ear.

Her answer is cut off as Justin calls her name and waves her to come back to the makeshift stage.

She turns to face me. "Don't go anywhere. I'll be right back."

When she walks away, my eyes are glued to her form. I can't believe how goddamn lucky I got. I remember kissing her all those summers ago. She'd surprised me then at the end of her vacation. We didn't get the chance to pursue anything because she left the next day to go to California. As time zoomed by, we never connected. I was in college, or she had a boyfriend, or I only saw her in passing. I never thought I'd have the opportunity to see what could be until now.

The kids are off the stage when Riley gets up there. Justin wraps an arm around her, tugging her close.

"When I heard Riley here was a part of the event, I knew I had to be a champion for the cause as well," Justin says.

One of the reporters holds up a hand, and Justin nods for her to ask her question. "What about the two of you? You were in a relationship a few months back? Are you together again?"

"Great question," Justin says. "Believe me, I've been thinking that very thing. What do you say, Riley? Is the dynamite couple back?"

I take a step forward before I catch myself. What am I going to do? Beat my chest and throw her over my shoulder? I can have private words with him later.

"It's dynamic," she says to Justin. I see her mouth form the word *idiot*, and I have to laugh. She aims her piercing gray eyes at the crowd. "And this isn't about us.

It's about these wonderful children. I don't have any of my own, but my heart goes out to the families that have to go through so much to battle what they do. That's what we're here for."

Another reporter, ignoring her comment, shouts, "You call yourselves a dynamic couple? Do you mean power couple?"

"They would make a perfect pair in golf," Randy says for my ears.

At the same time, Riley tries to say, "We are not—"

Someone else cuts her off, "Do you think marriage is in your future?"

"Absolutely," Justin says. "Last time we were here in May, Riley and I went to the corn festival to celebrate the harvest. It was delightful."

"Corn festival in May? They don't harvest corn here in May. It doesn't begin until mid-June at the very earliest," Riley mutters. "And we are not—"

"Do you guys still practice together?" It's another question from the crowd.

"She played better this year for it," Randy says to me.

Justin is saying, "I hope so. I have better hand-eye coordination when she's around."

The asshole winks and tries to rope his arm around Riley again. I can't watch anymore. I trust Riley, but between Randy and Justin, I need a drink. If I don't calm down, I'll end up making a scene. Somehow I think that'll be worse for my girl. I open my clenched hand.

"Are you ready to be Mr. Riley Wilde?" Randy asks.

My eyes narrow as they focus on him. "What are you saying now, old man?"

I've lost all decorum. Riley might hate me for this, but he's been trying to get a rise out of me for days.

"Are you ready to give up your career and follow her around the world to tournaments to support her?"

"I'll always support her."

"From afar? How long do you think that will last? Riley's a beautiful woman. And with her earning potential, some guy will be willing to give up his career to be there for her whenever and wherever."

"And what? You think that's you," I chide.

"Oh, I would be better for her because I know what it takes for her to be successful. But I have a family and would never dream of it. Besides, you'll never make the kind of money she makes. Will your ego handle that?"

A muscle in my jaw ticks as I try to bite off the nasty things I want to say. "You have no idea what I make or what I could make."

"In other words, no. You're going to find another job and make your career. You'll leave her to go at this game alone. And she'll do it. I see how she looks at you. But one day, she'll resent you for it. Or you her, if you give up your life for her. It will never work out between the two of you. Her career has to come first. And if you can't accept that, you should move on."

I don't bother saying anything else to Randy because I'm seriously ready to knock the shit out of him. Striding off, I send a text to Riley to meet me in the bar.

On the way, I get a call.

"Ben," I say into the phone and push back all my anger.

"When are you leaving our great state of South Carolina?"

Not soon enough, I think. "On Monday, I believe."

"Why don't you have dinner with my wife, Samantha, and me on Friday or Saturday?"

"As I mentioned, I'm here caddying for Riley Wilde. I'll need to check with her, but I think Sunday would be better. She'll be playing until then."

"Okay, let me know what day. We'll make it work. But I really want to give my final pitch before you leave. I have something else I want to put on the table that might sway you to say yes."

I chuckle. "You drive a hard bargain, Ben."

"I go after what I want. And I want you on our team."

"I'll get back to you after I talk to Riley."

"Sure, and you make sure to bring her with you if I didn't say that earlier."

Ending the call, I find a seat at the bar in the clubhouse.

"A whiskey, please."

By the time Riley shows up, I've had a couple. Her eyes are hard, and I know she's pissed. I sigh, ready for her verbal beating.

"You left me again. Is this going to be a pattern with you?"

I hold up a finger. "This time my motives were purely altruistic."

"How so?" she asks with her brows arched.

"I would have been arrested for hitting an old man and a dumbfuck. I didn't think you wanted that to be on *TMZ*." With air quotes, I add, "Jealous boyfriend beats up Riley Wilde's coach and former lover. See pictures below."

Her hand drops from her hip, and she looks less likely to throttle me.

"What did Randy say now?"

"Nothing I couldn't handle. But between the pair, I had to walk away or I'd need a lawyer."

She laughs. "I don't know whether to be mad or what?"

"Or what?" I say and take her wrist to pull her close.

Her mouth gives under mine. Just as I start to take it deeper, she pulls back.

"How much have you been drinking?"

"Not enough," I mutter and swallow the rest, emptying my glass.

"Let's get you back to the room. We have an early start in the morning."

I leave some cash for a tip on the counter and knock my fist to get the bartender's attention. He glances in my direction in acknowledgment. I get to my feet.

"You know I had a hard-on for you all day. I kept imagining fucking you on the green."

Playfully, she smiles up at me. "We can make that

happen."

"Fuck, Riley, don't tease me. I have no control when it comes to you."

She only laughs and loops her arm in mine to lead us to the front. We end up in the island van headed back to the hotel to my great disappointment.

"Oh, I forgot to tell you Ben called and wants to have dinner with us before we leave. I thought maybe Sunday night since you'll be playing until then."

"Is there any other time? Sunday night is the big gala. It's where all the major sponsors come in and present their checks. I wish there was some way I could work that out, but I can't miss that," she explains.

"You didn't tell me about that."

She frowns. "I'm so sorry. With everything else going on, I must've forgotten to tell you." Absently, she mutters, "Randy thinks I need to hire an assistant because I can't keep everyone in the loop."

I can't immediately think of a solution. "I have to see Rhoades. He wants to offer me something else."

"Can't he tell you over the phone?"

"This could be my future boss, Riley. The least I could do is meet him and his wife. And want you there with me."

"You know you're absolutely right. After everything you've done to help me out, I feel like shit that I can't make it. But you should go."

"Will the kids be there? At the gala?" I ask.

"Well, no, it's a black tie affair. But the press will. My

presence will be missed if I don't show up. Otherwise I would skip it and go with you."

"I didn't bring a tux. So I guess that settles it. I won't leave you stranded on the course. I'll go to dinner with Rhoades Sunday if it works for him. And you'll go to the gala without me because you need to be there, unless you can find time to have an earlier dinner with them another night?"

"Mark, I don't know. I don't make it a habit of going out on the evenings before I have to play."

"Gotcha. We'll work it out."

RILEY

This is the first time we sleep in separate beds since the night we arrived. I'm pretty damn upset with him. He knows this isn't a tournament and that it's a charity event, but the whole reason I'm here— we're both here—is to champion the Make-A-Wish Foundation. This is all about bringing in large sums of money to help these kids. The gala on Sunday is the closing event. I explain it to him until I'm blue in the face—or at least that's how I feel. The bad thing is, I see his side, too, and I really do want him to get this job. He deserves something this awesome. What a damn dilemma.

This is all my fault for not telling him about the gala. I thought I had, but I'll take the hit for missing it. Randy is probably right. I do need an assistant. There are way too many details in my life that need attention that I'm missing.

My poor pillow. I've beaten the shit out of it tonight.

It's better than punching the wall. Only I've gotten hardly any sleep. And tomorrow the real golfing begins. Randy will be on my ass, worse than he already is, and that dumbass Justin doesn't understand the meaning of *no*.

I give up on sleep well before the sun's up, shower, dress, and decide to sneak out to watch the sun rise. But I'm surprised to see Mark in the living room of the suite when I exit my bedroom.

"You're up early," he says.

"Yeah. You are, too."

He closes his laptop and says, "Couldn't really sleep either."

We both start to speak at once, and then kind of laugh. "You go first," I say.

"What I was going to say is that last night sort of got away from me. I'm sorry about that."

Shuffling my feet, I admit, "I'm sorry, too. Randy is right in that I need an assistant to keep some of my stuff from falling between the cracks. I can't keep up with it all. And it's no use for me telling you I mentioned everything to you when clearly I didn't."

Nodding, he asks, "What were you going to say?"

"Oh. I was going to ask if you wanted to join me outside for an early breakfast and we could watch the sun rise."

His gorgeous smile warms me. "I'd like that very much."

He's already had a shower, too, so we head to the hotel café and order a to-go breakfast of coffee and egg biscuits. Then we head out to the terrace that overlooks the ocean and watch the sun lighten the horizon.

"It's really something, isn't it?" I remark.

"I think so," he says, reaching for my hand.

Glancing over at him, I notice he's not even looking at the view, but staring at me instead.

"You're not even watching the sun rise, are you?"

"Nope. I have no reason to with you sitting next to me."

Is this the same man who I was so pissed at last night? How did I let that happen? But then he has to open his mouth and shatter my illusion.

"I think Randy is right. Maybe I shouldn't be your caddie—that I'm nothing but a major distraction for you. This is a time when you should be completely involved in your game, and with me around you can't be."

"What are you saying?"

"Exactly what you think I'm saying. Me caddying for you was a mistake. It's taken your head off the game and into the bedroom. And that's the last place it needs to be. Be honest with me. Wouldn't you agree?"

When I hesitate, he jumps right in.

"See. It's a hard point to argue with, isn't it?"

He didn't give me time to think things through, so I respond with, "That depends. What exactly did Randy say to you last night? And let me just say if you don't tell me, I'll ask him myself."

His smile promptly curves into a frown, and now he decides to look at the view of the sun coming up. A long and painful silence eats up the space between us, and even though I want to speak, it would be wrong of me to do so.

He eventually leans forward, elbows on his thighs, and rests his forehead in his hands. "It was pretty much a mess. He said I should put you first before my career. Though he felt if I did I would eventually resent you. But if I didn't and left you to travel the world and golf without me, you would resent me. But either way, one of us will end up resenting the other. And the more I think about it, I wonder if he doesn't make a good argument."

"You honestly believe that? That we can't figure this out between us?" He needs to give me an answer before I invest more of my time, and possibly my heart in him.

I watch as he leans back in his chair and bends his neck from side to side. Shaking his head, he says, "I don't know, to tell you the truth. I'm not sure how I feel. I'd like to think we can make this work. But we couldn't even make simple dinner plans without a fight. Then again, how will we ever know for sure?"

My stomach takes a triple twisting dive to my feet, but instead of gracefully entering the water, like you see in the Olympics, it pancakes on the bricked terrace, sending impulses of shattering pain straight to my heart. Something in the recesses of my mind told me this would happen, but I chose to ignore it, trusting in the belief that for once, a relationship could work. I was dead wrong.

"We can't ever know that." My tone is flat. Suddenly,

I've lost my appetite and my desire to watch the beauty of the sun rise.

"Riley, what's wrong?"

What's wrong? Everything, now, it would seem. Yesterday, I had so many hopes, and now, not so much.

Standing, I say, "You need to figure out what you can or can't handle." My voice now carries a bitter edge to it. And yeah, I'm a bit pissed. I tried to push him away at first, but he's the one who insisted.

"Wait. You're not being fair. It's not all about what I can or can't handle. This is about the both of us."

"No. That's where you're wrong. You let one man put ideas into your head, and now look where it's gotten us. And if that's what's going to happen every time someone mentions something like that, then maybe you're right."

Not wanting more of this conversation, I walk away before I say something totally mean and stupid. The last thing I want is to sound like that moron, Justin.

By the time I step into the elevator, the dark-haired devil is on my heels behind me. The doors aren't even closed before he starts in.

"Don't ever run away like that again."

"Or what?" I challenge.

"Or … I don't know. Just don't do it. You're the one who told me not to leave. You know damn well that's not the right thing to do. And you also know we do have a huge problem looming before us."

"I am aware," I snap. "But I, unlike you, don't let

102

others dictate what I want or don't want."

The doors whoosh open, and I step around him and out. Again, he's on my heels.

"Don't you want me to caddie for you?"

Stopping to a dead halt and turning so he has to grab on to me to keep from knocking me over, I stare at him eye to eye. "Of course I want you to caddie for me. That is, unless you don't want to do it, in which case I'll get Randy to carry my bag."

"I'm a man of my word. I came here to do a job, and I'll do it, dammit."

"Okay then," I growl, "but you'd better act right."

"What the hell is that supposed to mean?"

"It means that I have to play well and be sweet to those kids. If you're acting like an ass, then it'll put me in a funk and I won't be able to do either."

He snorts. "Seems to me you're the one acting like an ass."

My jaws clamp together and I swallow my snarky retort, grinding my molars instead. Who is this guy kidding? Me? The ass? I jam the key card into the slot and open the door. He knows I'm beyond pissed now by the way I'm banging doors and throwing things around.

"Riley, calm down. You need to get ahold of yourself."

The only things I need to get ahold of are Randy's and Mark's necks so I can squeeze the hell out of them and then talk some sense into the two of those rock heads, when they are almost unconscious and can't yap back. Men. UGH.

When I'm ready to go to the golf course, even though it's early, I look at Mark with a quirked brow.

"What?" he asks.

"You ready?"

"Now? It's barely daylight."

At least his rock brain noticed that.

"I realize that, but I'm going to the range to burn off this, er, energy I have." Translation: anger.

"Oh." He scrutinizes me. "You're really pissed off at me, aren't you?"

"You bet your sweet ass cheeks I am, Einstein."

"Don't you think—"

"No. If we discuss this any further, I won't be held liable for my actions."

He has the gall to laugh. And I'm talking a hearty howl. Oooh. My ass is burning now. I need to rein it in. How in the world am I going to play a decent round?

I stomp toward the door, and he says, "Calm it down a little, Eagle. It's going to be fine."

If he knew my blood pressure was about the same temperature as boiling water, he wouldn't be saying that.

"You know what? Why don't you just meet me there about thirty minutes before my tee time? Make it around noon. That'll give *Eagle* time enough to *calm down*. Oh, and just for the record, you and your doubts? Well, I believe in us and I'm willing to walk through fire to prove it." And I practically run out of the room, not looking back.

By the time I get to the elevator, I'm panting. What the hell is wrong with me? Before I know it, my feet have burned a path to the transportation desk.

"But miss, the golf course isn't even open yet," the poor little guy tells me.

"I know, but I want to go to the driving range."

"But, that's not open either."

"It's okay. I'm with the event. Someone there will let me on."

"Miss, I'm not supposed to do this."

"Please," I beg, using my best flirtatious voice. I'm much older than he is, but I know I've made an impression when he nods.

"I hope I don't lose my job."

"Listen, if anyone says anything, tell them Riley Wilde begged you to do it, and if they don't believe you, tell them to leave me a message in my room. I'll vouch for you."

That appeases him and off we go. The course is deserted when we arrive.

"Miss Wilde, are you sure you want me to leave you off here?"

"Yeah," I say, waving my hand. "I'm fine."

When he's gone, I plop on the bench that conveniently awaits me. The course will open in an hour, and until then I'm content to stay here and sort things out in my head. I'm sitting, enjoying the morning calm when my blissful peace is disturbed as that dumbass,

Justin, appears.

"Riley, what are you doing here?"

"I might ask you the same."

He chuckles and says, "I bribed one of the employees to bring me. I'm meeting my caddie here for an early breakfast, and then I'm going to hit balls before my tee time. I like the shotgun start at noon. What hole are you starting on?"

The man gets dumber and dumber every year. What did I ever see in him?

"Justin, no one knows which hole. They're making those determinations this morning."

His face contorts from confusion to clarity and I bite back a laugh.

"Aw, that's right. I always forget at these things. Maybe we'll start on the same hole."

If I were an eye roller, mine would roll right out of my head on his last statement.

"Justin, let's think this through. How many holes on the course are there?"

"Eighteen," he answers eagerly.

"Good. And how many golfers are here playing?"

"Eighteen."

"Boy, you must've studied up last night."

The dude actually preens a bit. What a doofus. "So?"

"So?"

Oh my God. Save me from his lack of brain activity. Surely his mother dropped him on his head when he was in infant. And sad as this may seem, it would be better if she had. At least there would be an explanation for his sheer idiocy. How could I ever have dated him? Was I that desperate? It must've been at a really low point in my life.

"So, Justin, what that means, is each golfer will be playing their own hole. We will all have some of the kids with us. It was intended to be that way so we could spend quality time with the kids."

"Well, what about spending quality time with the golfers."

"I give up. You'll have to ask someone else about that." I'm done giving important details to the guy who went to the corn festival in May when it doesn't even exist!

"Yeah, okay."

And he's fine with that. Checking my watch, I notice the course is about to open and decide it's time for me to head inside. But Justin's next words halt me.

"So enough about golf. Let's talk about us," he says. I have to remember this dude is as dense as a forest.

"Justin, there is no us. There will never be an us."

"Oh, but there is. You saw the media and how they were all into America's favorite golf couple."

He flashes his pearly whites as if he's acting in a tooth whitening commercial.

"Good for the media. Not so good for us. Let me repeat myself. There is no us, Justin. Get used to it."

I stand up and get ready to walk away, but he grabs my wrist. "I want us to give it another try."

"No! No trying, no nothing."

But he gives my arm a tug and it catches me off guard, so I take a bit of a tumble and end up catching myself with my hands on his lap. His lips are on mine before I can even think, and damn, if Randy doesn't show up at exactly that moment.

"Well, I didn't imagine catching you two lovebirds here," he says.

Pushing myself away from Justin, I say loudly, "Randy, it's not what you think. And, Justin, don't you ever put your hands on me again."

But when I turn to speak to Randy, he's disappeared. What the hell?

MARK

Rubbing my temples, I sit on the sofa wondering what to do next. I can run after her, but she's made it clear she needs to work off some steam. My phone buzzes in my pocket, and I answer it immediately.

"Riley?"

"Er, no. It's Gina. So don't say anything stupid."

I blow out all the air I've been holding. "Hey, what's up?"

"What's going on with you? You sound like you just found out Santa isn't real."

Part of me wants to confess everything to her, but her fiancé is Riley's twin brother.

"Nothing. It's early for you, isn't it?" I ask, switching subjects.

"Well, Ryder didn't get to see his sister play much this season, and he wanted to surprise her."

"So, you guys are here?"

"Yep. We're downstairs about to have breakfast, and we wanted to invite you guys down."

Great. They are going to ask questions I don't want to answer. "Riley's already gone." My answer is simple, and I can only hope Gina leaves it at that. But of course she doesn't.

"Trouble in paradise?"

"Gina, don't start."

"Fine Mr. Grumpy Pants. Come meet us. I have something I need to discuss with you."

I check my watch. There are still a few hours before the event begins. "Okay."

When I get downstairs, Gina hops out of her seat to greet me. Over her shoulder, Ryder glowers at me. I don't know if it's Gina hugging me or if she's told him that Riley and I are on the outs. No telling, it may be both.

"I missed you," Gina says into my ear.

"I missed you, too. How's New York?"

We let each other go, and she looks back at Ryder. "It's good." She indicates with her hand for me to use the chair opposite her. "Sit, sit."

As I do, I hold out my hand to Ryder. "Hey, man."

He grumbles something and begrudgingly shakes my hand using a vise grip. I give as good as I got. The Wilde twins must not be morning people.

"I ordered for you," Gina says. "Ryder wants to get out there and see Riley before everything gets started."

"It's fine. You know what I like."

Ryder's eyes narrow. "Do you have a problem with me?" I ask.

Gina sighs. Ryder answers, "Should I? What's going on between you and my sister?"

"Should I ask you the same?" I toss back.

"You don't have a sister," he counters.

"Gina's been like a sister to me forever."

"Is that before or after the two of you hooked up?"

"Ryder," Gina growls.

"Look, you've got to let that go. Fletcher, Cassie, Gina, and I grew up together. We went to the same schools. Gina was like one of the guys," I muse, memories flooding back. "Until she wasn't. We were teenagers. What happened, happened over a decade ago and more out of curiosity."

"And it was gross," Gina interjects.

"Thanks for the vote of confidence," I say to her.

"You know I didn't mean it that way. As I've explained to Ryder, it was like doing my brother and that's just eww."

"Exactly," I say, although I'd held a torch for her for a short time after. The point is, I'd been over her for a very, very long time. "And I stress again, it was once and done. If we can forget it ever happened," I point between Gina and me, "why can't you?"

"Well, if Gina didn't choose you, maybe you're not right for my sister."

Ryder's on a roll, and I'm his target. The guy's not spiteful either. Has Riley already talked to him?

I toss my hands up. "You know what? I don't need this bullshit today."

"Ryder, that was fucked up," Gina says.

I'm halfway out of my seat, but Gina snags my hand.

"Ryder," Gina warns.

"I don't need you to run interference for me, GG," I say, adding that last bit to piss Ryder off. And it works.

"GG?" Ryder growls.

Gina shrugs. "He's always called me that."

It isn't exactly true, but she has my back and I love her more for it.

"Please stay," Gina asks.

I turn to Ryder. "I get Gina's your girl. Hell, I championed for you. I thought you would be good for her. But I don't ask her about what goes on between the two of you. I don't expect you to ask me about your sister. She can handle herself… and me."

Ryder turns his attention to the view out the window for a minute. "You're right. Riley's always led the charge on her battles. I'm sorry. I've been under a lot of pressure, and I haven't had a lot of sleep. I shouldn't take it out on you. Yes, I'm a jealous bastard. But I trust Gina."

"And?" Gina prompts.

"And I trust you," he says to me.

He holds out his hand. This time the shake is friendlier.

"So, what happened?" Ryder asks again. I arch a brow. "I'm asking this time because maybe I can offer you some advice."

Tension eases as our food arrives. I give them a basic overview of my week with Randy. Then, I tell them the story of what happened with Randy and Justin."

"That's messed up," Gina says.

"Randy can be an overprotective fool. He's really a good guy when it comes down to it," Ryder adds.

"I get that, but he's crossed a line," I say.

"I'll say one thing. I don't think my sister wants some guy whose only life goal is to be her cheerleader. She'd walk all over that guy."

"But?" I ask.

"But Randy is partially right. It gets lonely when you travel. City after city in different hotel rooms..." He puts an arm behind Gina's chair. "To have someone be there after a tough day means a lot."

Gina smiles at Ryder and places her hand over his on her shoulder.

I envy their bond.

"I can see that," I say.

"Whatever job you take, will you be able to go to some of her tournaments especially if you can tell she needs you?" Ryder asks.

There is a lot to consider, and I do that over breakfast.

We are waiting on island transportation when I ask Gina, "You said there was something you needed to talk to me about."

"Oh," she says. Her face lights up, and her movements become animated. "Ryder and I are thinking about doing something a little different for our wedding."

"What's that?"

"Cassie is my maid of honor, and Fletcher is Ryder's best man," she begins.

"Yeah," I say because that isn't unexpected.

"Well, Ryder wants Riley to stand for him. And I want you to stand for me on my side."

I grin. "Do I have to wear a dress?"

She laughs. "No. A tux with the right color tie to match Cassie's dress works."

"Does Riley know? Will she be in a tux, too?"

Gina shakes her head. "Not yet. But I see her in a black dress to match the guys, and a sash of some sort to match our color theme. We want to break tradition. Ryder's mom will probably die." She snorts, and Ryder grins along with her. So no trouble there. "She'll probably ask why you can't be on Ryder's side and Riley on mine. But fuck tradition. This is our wedding."

I can't argue. Instead, I spend the whole time wondering if Riley and I will be together at their wedding, or apart.

"You know, maybe you should wear a kilt."

Ryder laughs, and I scowl. I hope she's not being serious. Nothing against Scottish tradition, I have some of that in my blood, but I've never worn one before.

We get to the exclusive club. It doesn't take long for us to find Riley. She's got a circle of kids around her. She's showing them how to putt on the mini green near the clubhouse that was made for kids.

When Riley sees Ryder, she hands off the kids to another female golfer. She hugs her brother like it's been years since they've seen each other. For a second I hope for that same smile when she finally notices me. Gina is next to get Riley's warmth. They talk animatedly, and so far Riley ignores me.

Finally, the conversation dies down. Justin emerges from the clubhouse and heads directly for my girl.

"Riley, can we talk?" I ask quickly.

She nods and I move over to her and place a hand on her back. I guide her past Justin who looks annoyed. We keep moving into the clubhouse. For total privacy, I usher her into a private bathroom.

"If you're still pissed at me, maybe Randy should caddie for you today," I say. "I don't want to mess with your game."

I said this earlier, but I need to make sure. She glances away, and my stomach sinks.

"You're giving up on me already?" she asks, finally locking eyes with me.

Relief floods me. I don't waste the air with words. Stepping up to her, I kiss the ever-loving shit out of her. That starts a fire between us. Her hand dips into my shorts and grabs my cock.

Curses leave my mouth. "We can't. I didn't bring any condoms."

"And I can't go play with my mind wrapped around your dick. You said you don't want to mess up my game."

She smirks at me.

"What are you saying?" I ask.

"I'm saying I've never had unprotected sex. You?" I shake my head. "Then fuck me, Mark, and now."

I glance around the small bathroom. There is a toilet and a sink. Not much else.

"Take off your shorts. Leave on your underwear," I demand.

She gives me a quizzical look, but does what I ask.

"Wrap your legs around my waist."

I help her up by her ass. Pressing her into the wall, I slide my dick out of my shorts. Then I push her underwear to one side. And I'm in. And holy hell. It's a whole different experience to be inside a woman bare.

"Shit, Riley, I'm pretty sure you've ruined me for anyone else. Now you can't leave me, like ever."

My brain short circuits then. It's a wonder I can make out her next words.

"Who said I was going anywhere? We'll figure this out."

All talking ceases as I begin to pump into her. I have to kiss her little cries and moans to hopefully ensure we don't get caught.

No matter how much I want this to go on for years, I'm not going to last minutes with her wet cunt squeezing the hell out of my cock.

She sounds like a sexy kitten when she purrs breathlessly, "I'm coming, Mark."

"Don't hold back, baby. Let go. I've got you."

Her pussy contracts around my dick and sets me off. I'm so lost I don't think about asking her a specific question until after we've come down from the high.

I'm holding her up with her arms around me and still balls deep inside her.

"Are you on the pill?" I don't stop there. Words pour from me. "Not that it matters. I'd give my fortune away to see you pregnant with my kid."

RILEY

"Isn't it a little late for that?" A happy giggle rushes out of me as he slides out.

"I did qualify it with my statement that followed." Mark grins like he won the lottery. So I comment.

"You didn't hit the jackpot, you know."

"That's for me to decide, and I pretty much think I did. But you never answered me."

I drag my lips across his and ask, "What was the question again?"

"Are you on the pill?"

"Oh, yeah. I am. No worries about any ankle biters."

"Ever?"

What's he asking me? "I'm not sure what you mean," I say.

He wraps his hand around my neck and asks, "Do you ever want any? Ankle biters, that is?"

"Maybe someday. Far off in the distant future. But it sure would be hard to stay on the tour being pregnant, and then with a little baby. Especially if I didn't want to leave."

"We could plan it out so you'd have the baby in the off season and hire a nanny."

What is he saying? He wants to have kids? "Um, Mark, I think we need to date first, you know. Get to know each other. Maybe get engaged, then marry. Isn't that the normal progression of things?"

The grin he flashes me is full of heat and sex. "Not always. There are plenty of people who have a few kids and then tie the knot."

Is he serious? He can't possibly be. "Wait. You want to have kids first?"

"You, barefoot and pregnant is beyond hot. I can't wait to see you when your belly button pops out."

"Hang on a second, mister. You need a willing partner in all of this, and I'm a little old-fashioned in the kid department. There won't be any kids until we're married."

"Hmm. So, you want to get married then? Is that what you're saying?" Now that sexy grin is cockier than ever. He had this whole thing planned all along.

"You're a sneaky bastard, you know that?" I poke him between the ribs. And I'm damn good at rib poking. I had a great teacher, namely my twin brother.

"Ow, that hurt!"

"That's what you get for tricking me like you did."

He laughs. "It was a pretty good trap, wasn't it?"

It's hard not to laugh with him. "Yeah, but you had

me there for a minute. I thought you wanted to knock me up and hang out for a while."

"Oh, I want to knock you up all right. But I'll do it properly, and when the time is right."

Wait. What did he just say? I pause, thinking this conversation through for a minute. I lift my eyes to his and find him staring at me, his gaze soft. All the kidding is gone, and there's something there that maybe I missed before, or was too busy chatting to notice. But his words, *I'd give my fortune away to see you pregnant with my kid,* plow into me. He *was* serious.

When I open my mouth to speak, he says, "Don't say anything. Not yet anyway. My mouth ran away from me, and because of that, I don't want *you* running away."

"Who says I'll run away?" I ask softly.

"Will you?"

"No."

And his mouth crash lands on mine right as someone knocks on the door. Fuck! I forgot where we were.

"We have to go," I whisper frantically.

He nods in agreement, as we both situate our clothing. When I reach for the door handle, he stops me. "Did you clean up? I didn't use a condom. I hate to break this to you, but you don't want my cum running down your leg during the match."

"Shit." He hands me some tissue, and I quickly do the task. Then I look up at him, and he grabs me and kisses me hard. "You can do this," he says.

"What? Win?"

"No, walk out of here and pretend I just didn't fuck the anxiety out of you."

I snort with laughter and open the door, to the shocked faces of two elderly women.

Mark puts his hand on my shoulder and says, "We're sorry. She had a wardrobe malfunction and needed my assistance." And he gives them a flirty million-dollar smile.

They nod, and one of them says, "Oh, dear. That happened to me once, and I had to back out of a tournament I was playing in. I couldn't keep my pants up."

"Such a tragedy, I'm sure," Mark says. "But we're all fixed here. I had to," and he leans forward and whispers something to them.

"Well, goodness, it's a good thing you were here, then," the other lady says. "Good luck to you. Hope you have a great round today."

I nod and smile as we walk off.

"What did you tell them?"

Mark chuckles. "I told them I had to help you hitch up your bra because the strap broke and there was no way you could play like that."

"Jesus, I wear a damn sports bra when I play."

He shrugs. "No worries. They bought it."

"I hope you can't see it through my shirt."

Mark leans back and announces I'm fine. We head toward the area where the other golfers are congregating, and Randy intercepts us with a huge, and I

121

mean huge, grin on his face.

"Boy, is the media waiting to pounce on you," he says.

"Why?" I ask. A deep suspicion forms in me.

Randy's smile fades as he shifts on his feet a bit. "They want photos of you and Justin."

Now that suspicion turns to anger. "And why would they want those, Randy?"

"I, uh, well, Justin may have told them a thing or two about you getting back together."

Seething anger displaces suspicion. "And why would he do that?"

Randy won't look me in the eye, which explains something. He had a hand in this. "That kiss you two shared, you know."

Mark's hand that was on my back is immediately gone.

"That little fucker. He's lying, and he trapped me. And what you saw wasn't what you think it was." I quickly turn to face Mark, and he's looking at Randy. When I glance at Randy, he looks exactly like the thief who's been caught red-handed.

Randy asks, "Riley, what did I see out there, then?"

Mark chimes in, "That's what I'd like to know."

Gritting my teeth, I say, "I lost my balance as the jerk grabbed my wrist, and he took advantage of the situation. He pulled me onto his lap and kissed me. There was nothing I could do to stop it, but we had heated words afterward. Unfortunately, Randy witnessed that and assumed the worst, but didn't stay for my explanation. And Randy, what I don't get is that you knew how I felt about him."

Mark stiffens, and his hands fist. Randy shrugs and says, "Justin made it sound like you reconciled."

Catching Randy's gaze, he knows I'm pissed. "And you went with that, without even checking with me."

Randy only shrugs, like it's not a big deal to him. "We'll get past this. We need to get you out on the course then."

"She's not going out there to be around that shithead," Mark says as he rises to my cause.

Randy waves his hand, saying, "Justin is harmless. He only wants the attention."

"And he may get some—more than he bargained for if he doesn't keep his hands off Riley." Mark turns to me and says, "Let's go," and he starts to usher me out the other door.

"Wait! You can't do that," Randy protests. "She'll miss all the publicity."

"As her caddie, I'll do what I think is best for her game, and right now, she doesn't need the distraction." His hand is on my elbow, steering me out of the room and away from the cameras, with Randy calling out my name.

When we get outside, I remember that Ryder and Gina are on the other side, along with my clubs. "You stay right here, and I'll take care of everything for you, Eagle." He leans toward me and runs his finger down my

123

cheek. Out of the corner of my eye, I see a dude with a camera lift it for a shot. Mark steps back before he snaps our picture. I chuckle.

"What's so funny?" I point in the direction of said picture taker. Mark grins and we pose for him, smiling, giving him some great shots. He even comes up to us, and we take some more close-ups.

"Hey, thanks, Miss Wilde. I hope you have the best round of your life today."

"Thanks. And will you post those pictures everywhere to dispel the Justin and Riley rumor? There is not and hasn't been a Justin and Riley for ages. It's Mark and Riley now. And you can quote me on that." The guy goes to leave, but Mark stops him and asks him to stay with me while he fetches my clubs, Ryder, and Gina.

"If you do this, I'll guarantee a family picture of the Wilde players."

"Man, that would be awesome."

While Mark is gone, I explain to the photographer what happened with Justin and how he "arranged" the accidental kiss. He lets me know he will pass it along to all his friends and be sure the other photos appear everywhere. It doesn't take long for Mark to return, along with Ryder and Gina, and we give the guy his promised photo session. At about the time we're finishing up, one of the clubhouse attendees drives around the side with a cart for us, but who shows up? Justin with Randy. What is it with Randy?

"There you are, sweetheart."

Ryder looks at me and scowls. Mark takes a step forward and goes into attack mode. I'm almost ready to say, "Down, boy." But I don't have to. Ryder beats me to the punch.

He steps between Mark and Justin and says, "Dude, my sister is only one guy's sweetheart, and I'm pretty damn sure it isn't you. So if I were you, I'd scurry along and get myself ready for the eighteen holes ahead."

But Randy isn't letting this go. "Ryder, I don't think you have all the details here."

"Oh, Randy, that's where I'm certain you are one hundred percent wrong. I usually don't speak for Riley, but I know her like no one else. That's the way it is with twins. She has no more interest in spending time with Justin than she does a squirrel gathering nuts, but go ahead and ask her if you want. Ri?"

"You're exactly right and, Randy, I don't know how else I can spell it out to you. Or to you, Justin." Then I turn to Mark and ask, "You ready to head to number five? I believe that's the hole I'm teeing off from, and I really want to spend time with my Make-A-Wish child and not debate this dead issue." Turning to Ryder and Gina, I hug them both and then ask them to follow me along.

"Wouldn't miss it for the world, sis."

Mark and I hop into the cart and head to number five. Usually, we walk during tournaments, but since this is a charity event and some of the kids are a little too frail to walk, they're having everyone drive carts. Once we hit the cart path, I thank Mark for standing up for me.

"What's Randy's problem?" He wants to know.

"I have no idea, but it may be time to find a new coach if he doesn't drop this Justin thing."

"Riley, I'm not sure it's Justin. I think it's me."

"I don't care. I'm the boss of my own life. I've hired him to help my game, and I appreciate his concern, but I'm not sixteen and can make good decisions."

Mark is quiet, and I'm not sure if it's because he's thinking about everything that happened or contemplating what I just said. Neither matters. I won't let him walk away from me without discussing things. Even if he thinks Randy may be right, and I know Mark and I will have obstacles, we'll have to deal with them and not avoid them altogether.

MARK

She's a wonder to watch. Not only is Riley stunningly beautiful, her heart is made of gold. More and more, I see what a wonderful mother she will be some day. And didn't that check off one of my boxes for a potential wife. I try to shake that thought away. I have to be crazy for thinking in those terms, except there she is giving her full attention to the family before her.

Today isn't about scores. It's about the families. Not every golfer is able step away from their competitive spirit, but Riley makes a point to include every member of the family at each hole. She sacrifices shot after shot so the kids don't feel as though they are lacking in any way. Her cheering as the child with terminal cancer hits the ball with what little strength he or she has makes me so damn proud she's mine.

A tug on my shorts has me glancing down. The youngest sibling glances up at me with wide eyes. I crouch down so she can speak to me eye to eye.

"Why aren't you playing?" she asks. "Do you not know how to?"

"I'm here to be Miss Riley's caddie." That's the name the kids were calling her. "Do you know what a caddie does?"

She shakes her head and keeps her eyes downcast.

"A caddie carries the clubs and gives advice as to what club to use."

Briefly, she raises her head. "Is that because boys are better than girls? At least that's what my brother says."

Her brother stands off to the side, petulantly swinging a club at the grass. Tufts of it spray with each hit. The country club staff is going to have a time repairing the damage. Although Riley has included everyone, when she works with each one individually, she gives that child her full attention.

"Boys are not better. I play golf, too, but if I play against Miss Riley, she'll beat me every time. And that's okay."

"Really?" she asks, eyes bright with possibilities.

"Really. Girls can do anything boys do, and better. Anyone can do well with practice."

"Even my sister?"

She points to the girl Riley is helping to take a swing off the tee. We were told in private by the parents they didn't think their older daughter would live out the year.

"Sure. With practice she will get better."

Delighted, the little girl darts off to share that news

with her brother. I watch him scowl as she shares that information. I head over before he has a chance to kill her joy with his bad mood. It might not be my place, but the parents are otherwise occupied at the moment. No one can begrudge them for giving their dying daughter a little more attention at the moment. It has to be very difficult to manage the three children given the situation.

"Hey," I say to the older boy.

He can't be more than eleven, I guess.

"Hey," he says sullenly, toeing the grass with his sneaker.

"You don't like golf?"

His eyes track to find his parents and sister. "It sucks."

It isn't the game he's talking about.

"It does. I can't imagine what your family is going through." He turns saucered eyes to me, and I can tell it's a relief to him that I understand. "I bet you have a lot of responsibility, especially with your younger sister." He nods. "That can be tough. But man-to-man, I'm sure you can handle it. You seem like a pretty tough guy."

He shrugs. "She's so annoying."

He glances over at the youngest sibling who has moved away to find a club of her own and is entertaining herself.

"I doubt she understands what's happening in the same way you do."

"She's always happy. Like doesn't she get it? Nobody at our house is happy anymore, but her."

Yelling isn't exactly what he did. He does, however, gain his family's attention. I wave and they take a second to ensure that their son's okay before going back to what they were doing.

"I bet your sister would appreciate the happy more than the sad faces. You can't want your memories to be filled with sadness. This is an awesome day. You get to play with the pros. And Riley's one of the best."

"She's a dumb girl," he mumbles, taking about my girl.

"She's definitely not dumb, and she can play better than most guys I know." Then I point off to the side. "You see that guy there."

His face lights up in recognition. "That's Ryder Wilde, one of the best pitchers in the game. He got traded to New York, though."

"Well, he's her brother. And one thing he never said to her was that he was better than she was in anything. In fact, he said that Riley can play every sport, probably better than he can."

"He did?"

I'm not sure of the exact conversation Gina shared with me, but I'm close.

"Absolutely. He encourages her and never makes her feel like she isn't good enough. And now, she's one of the best golfers in the world."

I don't clarify female golfers because I firmly believe that Riley can beat at least some of the men on the professional circuit.

"Why don't we go help your little sister with her swing?"

By the next hole, the boy is more engaged. He asks Riley if her brother would sign a ball for him. Riley glances at me, and I shrug. After she helps him and his youngest sister on their tee shot, with their parents' permission, I walk them over to where Ryder and Gina stand behind the ropes.

"It looks like you have a fan," I say, before the boy starts talking a mile a minute to Ryder.

Gina smiles at me. "And who do we have here?"

She bends down to the little girl's level. The girl's hand tightens in mine.

I follow and squat down, too. "She's going to be the next golfer or…"

"I want to play football," she says with confidence she didn't have before. "My daddy likes football."

Gina laughs. "That's awesome. I wanted to play, too, when I was your age."

"You did?" The little girl is amazed.

Gina nods, and I say, "And now she rides a motorcycle instead."

That starts a fury of questions.

By the time the day is done, the Wildes have made fans for life. After we say our final goodbyes, Riley leans her head on my shoulder.

She yawns. "That was fun."

"It was. You were incredible. No, you are incredible."

I kiss the top of her head, keenly aware of the

paparazzi nearby.

"You're just saying that to get laid. You have to know by now, I'm a sure thing."

She yawns again. I lift her up, cradling her in my arms, not caring if we get caught on camera. She's dead on her feet.

"What are you doing?"

"Don't argue with me, Eagle. Give me my five minutes to be your hero."

Her giggle is cute, and she sounds drunk with weariness and lack of sleep. "Can you fly like Superman or spin webs like Spiderman?"

I shake my head. "I'm more like Batman or Ironman. I can afford the toys I need to keep you safe."

She laughs. "And what toys are those? Your joystick?" But her eyes close and I'm forced to keep my response to myself.

On the way back to the hotel, Justin has somehow managed to squeeze in with us. The twerp keeps giving me the stink eye like he's twelve as Riley slumbers on my lap curled around me. I ignore him, secure in the knowledge she's mine.

My girl wakes when the van comes to a stop at the hotel. She insists on walking under her own power. That's my woman, strong and independent. Ryder snags his sister off to the side to talk. Our rooms are on different floors, and I give them a minute to catch up.

"So." I turn and see Justin casually stand next to me like we're old friends. "You may have won today, my friend, but I'll win the war."

The twelve-year-old in me that's dying to win this spitting contest eagerly wants to dispute the friendship comment. I manage to shove that boy back in the recesses of my mind.

"How so?" I ask smugly, because the war has already been won in my book.

"I was talking to my friend yesterday." He rattles off the name of the number one golfer in the world. "He's a fan of Riley's. He wasn't able to attend this week due to a family wedding. But he knows one of the best caddies who just became available and is looking for work and would love to come this weekend and help out Riley. In fact, he should already be here."

He fucking smirks at me as I do my best to keep it together by grinding my teeth and saying nothing. Riley has stopped talking to her brother, and she stares confusedly in our direction. Justin takes that moment to go to her and give her the news. Riley's face morphs from annoyance, to bafflement, to utter delight. And can I blame her? She has the opportunity to work with one of the best-known caddies in the world.

My phone buzzes. I see it's Rhoades and answer it.

"Ben, how are you? I've been meaning to call."

I turn away, not wanting to watch Justin talk to my girl, but I don't leave.

"Just wondering if you'll have time to think about having dinner with us before you go."

With everything, I hadn't decided what to do. On the

fly, I make a decision.

"I think maybe Friday night will be good."

Then I can still go to the gala with Riley.

"Will you bring that gorgeous golfer?" he asks. "Ow." Then he mumbles something I can't hear. "Sorry, my wife took offense to my choice of adjectives."

I laugh, imagining the thump to the chest he'd probably received. "It's unlikely Riley will come."

Ben, not one to give up, says, "Then pick a night when she can join us."

And here's the rub. Riley's made it clear to me her position.

"Her schedule is tight. So it will be just me."

"That's too bad."

"Don't like my company, Ben?" I joke.

"I wanted to bring Samantha and didn't want her to be bored with our conversation."

We set a time, but I tell him that I'll confirm tomorrow. That will give me a chance to talk to Riley about it again. It's not like she'll need me on the course if she accepts this new caddie Justin's set up. If she has a late tee time that day, I'll duck out in time to make dinner.

"I can't believe you're letting that ass win," Ryder says.

When had he walked over?

"Yeah, Mark," Gina says, the two of them gang up on me.

"He's offering her, professionally speaking, the

equivalent of something she shouldn't refuse. I'd be an asshole if I tried to interfere."

I tell them what Justin told me. Ryder nods and says nothing more. When Riley waves me over, I say goodnight. She doesn't speak yet, just holds my arm with other people in the elevator. However, it's easy to tell she's vibrating with energy she didn't have before.

Once our suite door closes behind us, she attacks me. Her hands draw my face down.

"I've been waiting for this all night."

The kiss is hungry, and food is last on either of our minds. She slips one of her hands to my chest and then it's around my cock. Just that quick, I'm instantly hard.

"Waiting, huh?" I growl. "I'll show you what you do to me when you make me wait more than twenty-four hours to have that sweet pussy of yours."

We tear at each other's clothes. She gets tangled in something, and we go down. But that doesn't stop her. So I don't let it stop me. I think I rip her shirt and her underwear. It doesn't matter when my cock finds home. I bury myself balls deep inside her.

Her back arches, and her nails score my skin.

"I'm going to fuck you so hard no other man's name will ever cross your lips again."

And I do just that. She repeatedly screams my name until a knock can be heard on the door only five feet away.

RILEY

"Who the hell could that be?" Mark asks.

"I don't know. Don't answer it. Maybe they'll go away."

He nuzzles my neck and whispers, "Not likely. With the way you were screaming my name, I'm sure they could hear you in the lobby."

My face heats. "That bad?"

"Oh, baby, it wasn't bad. It was hot as fuck." Then he grinds his pelvis against mine, which produces a moan from me. "That's right."

The knock turns into a pounding, and a voice calls out from the other side, "Riley, open up."

"Are we ever going to get rid of that fucker? He's like a feral cat that keeps coming back for food scraps."

"Hey, I'm not scraps," I say, slapping him on the ass.

"I wasn't referring to you." His mouth nips at my lips.

Wham, wham, wham. "Riley, I know you're in there. I heard you."

Mark rolls off me and helps me up. "Come on, Eagle. Let's get this over with so we can enjoy the rest of our night in peace."

We scramble around for our clothing, but I end up having to get a different shirt. "You ruined this." I laugh as I show him.

"I'll buy you a new one. Hurry. The creature is restless. He's probably going to meow in a minute."

I can't help but snicker as I hunt down a T-shirt to throw on. When I open the door, I'm surprised and not just slightly embarrassed to see Justin isn't alone. But I'm not the only one who's red-faced. Justin looks like a tomato out of my mom's garden, and the guy he's with is even worse.

"Riley, I'd like you to meet Wade McClary. Wade, meet Riley."

Fuck my life. It's the caddie Justin was telling me about.

"Wade, it's great to meet you. I've heard nothing but awesome things about you. Come in."

I usher them inside and introduce him to Mark. "Wade, this is my boyfriend, Mark." They shake hands, and Mark breaks the awkward ice with one sentence.

"Sorry it took us a minute to answer. Riley had me tied up."

Wade laughs, and Justin scowls. I grin and glance at the area where I tied him up, and then I notice my torn panties lying there. Fuck! How did I miss those?

Wade spies them at exactly the same time I do and says, "Oh, I think I see what she tied you up with."

Mark follows his gaze to the floor, bends down, and snags them, then stuffs them into his pocket. "Honey, I told you to pick up after yourself," he says with a wink.

"Uh, yeah. Right then. So, Wade, I hear you're available for hire?" Now my face is redder than the coals in a fireplace.

"That's correct. That is, if your boyfriend is willing to give up the reins."

Mark sidles up next to me and puts his arm around me. "I want to set the record straight here. I stepped in for Riley because she was in a bind. There's one thing and only one thing I want, and that's what's best for her. If she wants you as her caddie, then that is her decision to make, not mine."

That's the nicest thing he could've said. Not caring a damn who is in the room, I turn in his arm, saying, "That means more to me than I can possibly say. Thank you." Then I kiss him. Heat fires between us, and a tiny peck turns into a little more than I planned.

Someone clears their throat, so Mark pulls away and offers an apology. "Sorry, guys. I can't refuse a kiss when my girl offers one."

Wade says, "I don't blame you one bit. I'd do the same."

Mark glares at him. Wade quickly adds with his palms in the air, "I meant if my wife did that. I'm a happily married man. No worries on my account."

Justin has been suspiciously silent, so I take a peek at him and he is scowling at Mark, who's is in heaven. I'd laugh if we were anywhere else.

Mark relaxes at Wade's comment and adds, "You

seem like the perfect fit then. To be honest, I'm out of my league here, aren't I, babe?" he asks me.

"Oh, I don't know. You've done an amazing job so far. I wouldn't mind keeping you around."

"Did I say I was going anywhere? I'll be right here, by your side." He gives me a squeeze.

Justin finally opens his mouth. "Is this love-fest about over because I've had about as much of this as I can take?"

"Hmm," Mark says. "Love-fest. I like the sound of that." He's totally gloating now, and Justin looks as though he could chew through steel. The testosterone flowing in this room is through the roof.

"Wade, let's talk business. How about we sit over there?" I motion to the sitting area, thinking Justin will leave. But he tags along and now I'm more than a little annoyed.

Even though I appreciate Justin looking out for me, he can't be present during this business discussion. "Justin, thanks so much for the introduction to Wade, but we need to discuss business now."

ShitForBrains doesn't take the cue. Wade gets it as he eyes each of us uncomfortably. Finally, Mark steps in and says, "Look, man, what she's trying to say is she needs to discuss personal business with him."

Justin glowers at Mark. "I think I'm better qualified for this discussion than you are."

Oh, boy. This is not good. But Mark acts like the gentleman he is. "While that may be true, you won't be a part of her personal business discussions. Now, I'll kindly ask you to leave."

Justin shifts from one side to the other and stares at me.

"Justin, please. You're overstepping here," I say.

"Yeah, you kind of are." This time it's Wade speaking.

Appearing properly chastised, Justin heads to the door, but before he opens it, he says, "Riley, that guy is all wrong for you, and you know it."

I can't help myself when I ask, "Who, Wade? Then why'd you bring him here? He's supposed to be one of the best in the country."

"Not Wade. Mark." And he jabs his finger in the air toward my guy.

"Oh, I'd have to disagree with you there. Mark is pretty damn perfect for me. Have a good evening, Justin." A snicker leaks out of me as I look at my guy.

When the door slams, Mark says, "You're a bad girl."

"I'm sorry." It was a shame they had to witness that exchange.

"Don't be on my account."

Wade adds, "It's a little difficult to get a message across to him, isn't it?"

Mark chuckles. "You noticed, huh?"

Wade shakes his head. "I practically begged the guy to call you first instead of barging up here. Sorry for that. But when he wouldn't leave, well, that's was really weird."

"Not if you know Justin. He still thinks we're an item."

Wade's eyes go as round as a golf ball. "So, it's true then?"

"What?" I ask.

"The rumors about his less than stellar intelligence. My buddy is sort of a friend of his. And I use that term loosely. He's been burned by Justin a few times only because of some stupid things he's done, which I won't go into. But when he started to join us for this talk we're getting ready to have, I was going to ask him to leave."

Mark says, "I like you already, Wade, and we've known each other for what? Five minutes?"

Wade laughs. "Yeah, something like that."

"This is great. You being down here this weekend," I say. Then I quickly glance at Mark, "Not that I don't appreciate everything you've done for me." And I do. He's been more than awesome.

"Oh, I'm cool with this. If you find a caddie that works for and with you, that's the greatest thing. I'm all about your game," Mark says.

I laugh. "He says that because he knows a well scoring golfer is a happy golfer."

"I get that," Wade says.

"Then let's talk business. This weekend is perfect for you to start. It's not tournament play so you can sort of get a feel for what I need. And there's no pressure because I'm spending a lot of time with the kids."

"That's exactly what I was thinking. I can read your

drives and putts, and then we can confer afterward. I have to tell you I've watched your career take off, and your skills impress me. I'd love to see them do a match where they'd pair up some women and men. You could take some of the men pros."

"Oh, I don't know." Ryder's told me as much, but he's a baseball expert, not a golfer.

"Stop with the modesty," Mark says. "If you're going to play, you need to own it."

"He's right, Riley. It's okay if I call you Riley, isn't it?"

I laugh. "Of course. I can't imagine you calling me anything else. Besides, there'll be days you might want to call me bitch or worse."

Everyone laughs.

"I guess this is the part where we negotiate the money," I say.

"Tell you what," Wade begins. "Why don't we do this? Let's get through this weekend. Since there isn't a purse, this one will be on me. You won't owe me anything. We'll see how compatible we are, whether or not we'll make a good team. If we think we can work well together, we'll go back to the table and discuss a contract. How does that sound?"

"Too good to be true," I say.

Mark has been sitting here listening in, but he perks up and asks, "Do you mind if I ask you something?"

"Not at all," Wade answers.

"Why'd you leave your other golfer?"

Wade stiffens. "I'll be honest, but I can't tell you

much because I signed an NDA. Let's just say we had a huge difference of opinions that involved moral ethics."

"I see." A gigantic grin covers Mark's face. I think Wade and I will get along just fine.

"One thing, Wade. Do you know who my coach is?"

"Yeah, Randy?"

"Uh-huh. He tries to interfere a little too much in my personal life. I want to make sure that doesn't happen between us."

Wade shakes his head. "What you do off the course is your business. However, if it is unethical, I will be obliged to resign."

Waving my hand, I say, "You won't have a thing to worry about in that regard."

"Good to know."

We all stand and walk toward the door. "So, what time do you want to meet in the morning?" Wade asks.

"Eight is good. They have a breakfast in the clubhouse for the players and all the guests."

"Sounds great. I'll see you there." A round of handshaking takes place, and then he leaves.

Mark smiles, saying, "This couldn't have turned out any better for you."

"Right? Although I'm pretty sure it's not the way Justin planned."

Mark bursts out laughing. "Not at all. That guy has nothing but air between his ears. He was going to plop his ass down over there while the two of you chatted up business. And he didn't see anything wrong with that."

"I know. Wade was pretty damn funny about all that, too. You're not upset about not being my caddie, are you?"

He grabs me and pulls me into the circle of his arms. "Not at all. I'm happy for you. Wade is exactly what you need. But I need to talk to you about something. Rhoades wants to meet me for dinner."

I can't begrudge him this. He has his career, and he can't let it slide away because of me. I need to figure out how to deal with this. "Okay, when?"

"I told him I needed to work it around your schedule. He really wants you to come, but I explained how tied up with everything you were."

My heart just melted, like a Hershey's Kiss on a hot summer's day. He's putting me first, and I have to ask myself if it's really fair.

"Maybe I can somehow work it out to go with you. Like after Sunday, since that's when the gala is. From then on we'll be done. What if we stayed Monday and met them that night for dinner? Would that work?"

"I can check, but this is your weekend, not mine."

"It's not like that. We're a team, Mark, and we need to start looking at it like that. Some days it'll be impossible for me to be there for you, but I can work this out, if Rhoades is willing to do it."

"He did want his wife to join us, so maybe he'll go for Monday."

Smiling, I lean in for a kiss. "And that would give us an extra day here, just to relax."

"I'd like that."

He nuzzles my neck and hits that spot, the one that makes me want to drop my panties and scream. But damn, if there isn't another knock on the door.

"Riley, open up. You've had enough time alone." It's Ryder. "Crap."

"Can't blame him for wanting to hang out with his sister."

"I want to get laid, though."

"Want me to tell them to give us a few?" he asks.

"No," I pout as I go to open the door.

Ryder barrels into the room, followed by Gina. "What has you frowning?" He wants to know.

"Too many interruptions. First Justin and now you."

"Justin? What the hell did he want?"

Then I grin. "I got a new caddie. His name is Wade." I go into the whole damn story, and by the time I finish, Ryder wants to know if I'm hungry. I am, but not for food.

Mark says, "Yeah, let's go eat."

As we're heading down the elevator, I remind him to call Rhoades.

"Who?" Ryder asks.

"We'll tell you at dinner." We walk into the restaurant, and who is sitting there? None other than Randy and Justin.

Gina asks, "Do you want to leave?"

"And go where? This is the only restaurant in the hotel. And I'm fine."

Mark puts his arm around me as we are escorted past their table to ours. Randy stops me and says, "I hear you got yourself a new, more qualified caddie."

This burns my ass but good. "Yes, Randy, but Mark was doing me a huge favor, out of the kindness of his heart. You seem to keep forgetting that." Mark's fingers give my waist a squeeze.

"Maybe, maybe not."

"What's that supposed to mean?" I ask.

"What that means is, perhaps he had ulterior motives."

"Such as?" Mark asks.

"You don't have to ask me that. You should know, since they're yours," Randy says.

"Okay, I've had enough of this. Randy, you treat me as though I'm twelve."

"Riley, this man is going to ruin you, if you let him."

"I think you have it all wrong. *You're* going to ruin me, if I let you. Randy, if this doesn't stop, I may be forced to find a new coach."

"You don't mean that."

"Yes, I do. I'm tired of all the underhanded comments. Just stop."

We get to our table. Ryder and Gina didn't see or hear what happened, as they were in front of us. As soon as we get there, Ryder asks, "What the hell happened?"

When he hears the whole story, he wants to deliver a couple of well-aimed punches to two guys. "Randy's being a dumbass."

"That's because he's been hanging around Justin, listening to him run his stupid mouth. And that makes no sense to me because he never really cared for the man."

"Randy doesn't like me is why he's doing that. So, what are you going to do?" Mark asks.

"If Randy doesn't stop, I'll start the search for a new coach. I can't deal with this anymore. I have too much on my plate as it is. The problem is, most of them are in Florida and aren't flexible about coming up to North Carolina. That could be problematic for me. But I'll figure it out. "

Mark reaches for my hand, and it's nice to know he's here. But after all the years I've spent with Randy, his behavior toward Mark stings like a mother. Justin swayed him, and his loyalty should've been with me.

MARK

" "Why don't we take a walk?" I suggest.

"Are you serious? I've walked all day."

"I know, but it's a nice night. And we only have a few more left."

I take her hand. She tugs a little against me, but it's only halfheartedly. The night air is like a balm, and with her hand in mine, the possibilities of the future seem endless. And what am I thinking? Future? Is it too soon? I push the thoughts away as we head out the back, and all the noise of the clubhouse disappears.

"Where are you taking me?"

Her voice is sexy as hell, and my dick stirs in my pants.

"Like I said, for a walk."

She stops. "It's a beautiful night, but honestly, Mark, I'm tired. I just want to curl in bed next to you."

There is promise in her words, one I'm counting on.

"Then I'll have to carry you."

I scoop her up in my arms to squeals of her delight. My destination isn't far. The only hole with enough cover that's not marsh is the first one. A small line of trees is to the left of that, and I step past the tree line. I set her down, and she immediately surveys the area as if she hadn't paid attention as I carried her here.

"Why are we here?"

But she knows. The way she says it is almost a playful challenge.

"I think you know why."

Her voice goes husky, perking my dick up further.

"Tell me then," she says.

Her arms cross over her chest, lifting her perfect breasts. My mouth waters at the sight.

"This is where it all started today," I begin.

"What started?"

"My dick. All day, I've been hard watching you play. I could hardly think outside of wanting to toss you to the ground and fucking you hard."

Her brow lifts in a perfect arch.

"Is that so?"

I take her hand and press it to my cock, which is like a lead pole in my pants.

"What do you want me to do about it?" she slyly says.

So many things come to mind. All day I've pictured her naked and me inside her.

"I want you to get on your knees and blow me." I expect a challenge, so I add, "You're the one who said your feet hurt."

With her chin lifted, she doesn't back down as if I double-dared her to do it. Slowly, she bends to her knees, then works at my belt. As soon as my zipper is down, my dick springs free. She doesn't waste time. Her mouth is warm and wet. When she takes me in, I'm about undone.

"Fucckk." The word comes out as a long moan.

Her teeth graze lightly over me as a wicked expression appears on her face. I know she's doing it on purpose, the little minx. I cup the back of her head and pull her forward, feeling myself hit the back of her throat. It doesn't stop there. She swallows and then takes me down further. Her eyes begin to go glassy in the moonlight, so I pull back. She blinks back the tears before drawing me back in without so much as a gag. I like fucking her mouth, but the more she teases me, the more I need to taste her.

With her cheeks hollow, my cock comes free with a slight popping sound. I hoist her up and help her out of her skirt-short thing. Bare to me, I lift her. She starts to wrap her legs around my waist, but I boost her up higher, using the tree for balance. I urge her legs to hook over my shoulders as I bury my face in her pussy.

She whimpers and moans as I suck and lick, lick and suck. Pussy like hers was made to be eaten. There's no acquired taste needed. I can't get enough of her. Her fingers dig in my scalp, grabbing fistfuls of hair as she calls out my name before coming on my tongue.

Pliable now, she's unable to help me as I slowly lower her after taking a step back from the tree. Once her sexy cunt is above my waist, I plunge into her.

"Damn, Eagle." I pause for a second, just enjoying the moment. "You feel so fucking good."

She doesn't answer me. Instead, her lips crash down onto mine, silencing anything that can be said in favor of a kiss that feels like tomorrow won't exist.

At some point we come up for air and I ask, "Can you stand, baby?"

She nods. Achingly, I pull out. I set her on her feet and spin her around.

"What are you doing?" she asks, not sure what I have planned.

"Hold on to the tree."

Her smile is like moonlight in a cloudless midnight sky. Compliantly, she turns and that's a little too easy. But then, she grabs ahold of the tree and bends a little. She taunts me by shaking her ass in my direction.

"Keep doing that and I'll think you want to play."

"Play," she jokes, glancing at me over her shoulder. "I thought you were going to punish me for teasing you all day."

I can't suppress the growl that leaves my throat. "So, you are teasing me?"

She winks, and I thrust. I'm inside her so fast I'm not sure which of us is more surprised. Her gasp ends in a moan, and I groan as well. This angle is always the best. I feel like I'm in unexplored deep space that chokes the hell out of dick. My pace is ruthless, and I hold her hips to keep her on her feet. Bending over her, I cup one breast as I squeeze her hip. Then I slide my hand to the apex of her thighs to circle her clit. Her breathy pants increase, which sends everything to the next level.

"I want to come," she cries.

"Don't worry, Eagle— you'll get your due. I'm not going for par tonight. I'm going for a hole in one."

She giggles as I wanted her to, but now it's time for the finale.

Rubbing my thumb over her clit, once then twice, and she's soon crying out. I shoot inside her like a geyser going off. When I slide out, my seed spills down her leg, and it's the sexiest thing I've seen, like I've marked her as mine.

I've come prepared. I pull one of the cloth napkins I hijacked from dinner to wipe her up.

She sighs. "Such the gentleman you are."

"I try to be," I say before kissing her and shoving the napkin into my back pocket after pulling my pants up.

"They've always said golf was a gentlemen's game, and I guess they're right because you certainly are." She winks.

Chuckling, I'm not surprised that I want her again. I always want her. I help her get dressed, and she continues to smile, but I can tell she's tired.

"I should get you back. You do have a golf match to win."

"For the kids," she says. "Though I think you're going

to have to carry me. I'm dead on my feet."

Noise of a golf cart stops me from making a sarcastic remark. We shift deeper in the shadows. A pack of people swerves to a stop near the first hole and us.

"Justin, you shouldn't be drinking and driving," a woman says.

Justin hops out and moves to stand in front of the headlights. Seeing him clearly now confirms who he is. He takes a long swig from a bottle he holds.

"Ladies, this is where the magic happens and where we should make our mark. And now you see why I bribed the maintenance guy for the cart with the headlights."

"Once again he's tossing his money around to get his way," Riley whispers.

He's a little too jovial, and most definitely drunk.

"Go away, Justin," Riley whispers to herself.

I agree. We're in an awkward position. If we leave, he'll see us.

A blonde comes around and shoves Justin to lean on the front of the cart. Drunk on his feet, he's easily pushed around. When she disappears, there's no doubt what service she's about to perform. Another woman pulls Justin's head back so she can kiss him from her position still in the front seat of the cart.

"Get your sweet ass out here and sit on my face," Justin orders.

Riley turns and groans into my chest. "Should we go? They might not see us," she whispers.

That's when I see a third woman yank off her shirt.

Even though it's dusk, it's not difficult to miss the outline of her too large to be so perky tits as Justin grabs a handful. I'm about to tell Riley let's make a mad dash for it when several flashes break the dim light.

"What the fuck," Justin says, expressing what we are all thinking. Riley turns in my arms to see as well. Apparently, the paparazzi have followed, hoping for the shot of a lifetime. And boy does Justin give them just that.

Spitting mad, he curses as the women gather and straighten their clothes. And Riley does something that surprises the shit out of me. She moves out of my arms and stalks forward.

"Justin, oh my God! What are you doing?" she cries out in a voice I've never heard before. Its tone sounds full of disappointment and regret, but something's slightly off for my discerning ears. She has to be putting on a show. "How could you do this to me? To these poor children here who look up to you?"

Even I feel sorry for the poor guy as Riley boxes him in opposite the cameramen.

"Riley," he says, sounding more dumbfounded by her presence than anything else. "I can explain."

"Explain? I think an explanation is unnecessary," she cries out.

It's the first time I wonder if Riley's chosen the wrong profession. Her acting ability is off the charts. She throws a hand up to place at the top of her head like she's about to faint.

"Why, you're nothing but a low-down dirty dog. And after everything you said this week. How could you? I thought—" She waves her hand in front of her face, as though she's going to cry.

Justin turns away and toward the flashing lights as I bite my lip, enjoying the spectacle, but not wanting to laugh. I know I have to leave my cover while everyone is distracted.

"Oh, woe is me. Why I never," Riley says in an exaggerated Southern drawl. She fans herself faster. I watch her profile as I head in her direction. She turns toward me and away from the cart. She bites her lip before turning back to her performance. "I can't believe that woman..." Her hand fans harder as if she's choked up. "...her mouth, Justin...how could you let her mouth be on your..."

Then Riley's knees buckle. It's as if she felt me close enough, because I'm there to catch her. Flashes go off like we are on the red carpet.

"Mark, please take me from this horrible place. I ... I just don't think I can stay here a minute longer."

I nod, because if I speak, I'll crack up.

"And Justin," she calls out. "Don't ever call me again. We are through forever."

If anyone catches an audio version of this, they will know Riley was acting. She doesn't have a Southern accent, having grown up in California, and her pretending one is off the charts.

"Was I good?" she whispers.

I nod, seeing the mischievousness in her expression. I hurry to get her back to the room.

Naked in bed, with her spooned up against me, I slip inside her. Slowly, we rock together. Her fingers tangled in mine as I squeeze her perfect breasts. I take my time, wanting it to last forever. I've never had such a connection with another woman. The idea of not having that has me tightening my hold around her, never wanting to let go.

As I come inside her, in a place somewhere deep within, I wish she weren't on the pill. I wish that we were planning a future and that I was planting a seed in her belly that would grow to be half of me and half of her. Only reality sets in.

Days fly by. The event ends with a staggering number of donations and pledges. It's a true success. Riley wins and Justin doesn't return after that night on the course. The scandal has him feigning an illness. He does, however, make a large donation to the event, which settles some ruffled feathers. Riley gives few answers to reporters, just saying that she and Justin never truly reconciled, but that it's over for good.

Sunday night, I stand in the room fiddling with my tie. Fletcher and Cassie arrived last night. He'd stopped by my place in Asheville and brought my tux for the gala tonight. Being the number one quarterback in the NFL right now, he'd easily secured invites for tonight's festivities. His support of the event will bring more awareness, just like Ryder's.

"What are the girls doing in there?" Fletcher grumbles, moping around. "This is our first night out."

His parents are in a room a floor below us with their slumbering child.

"Speaking of which, how's my godson?"

"The little cock blocker you mean," Fletcher says, but there is no real bite in his words.

There's so much pride on his face.

"That bad?" I ask.

He nods. "I don't think I even remember what pussy looks like."

Cassie walks out. "And if you keep complaining, you'll never see mine again."

Well trained as he is, he buttons his lip.

"Say it isn't so," Ryder says. "She's truly got you on a leash."

"I'd keep quiet if I were you," Gina says, entering the room next, protective of her best friend. "I could suddenly develop cramps."

Ryder clamps his lips shut. I'm about to laugh when Riley steps out of the room. And just seeing her takes my breath away.

RILEY

Mark stares at me as though his eyes have been shot out of his head like bullets. Waltzing up to him, I stick my finger under his chin and push it up, closing his mouth. Then I lean into him and whisper, "Like what you see?"

Stepping back, I wait for his response. His tongue drags a trail of wet across his lips, and I instantly want to pull him into the bedroom for a lazy fuck. It's even worse when I watch his Adam's apple bob as he swallows.

"You ... you're wearing that?" he finally chokes out. "No."

My brows draw together, and I immediately glance at Gina. She's the one who suggested it. She swore Mark would love it, and I took her word. When our eyes meet, there's more than merriment in hers. Gina is loving this. I get her nod of approval, only I'm not sure where to go with it.

I decide to find out exactly why he doesn't like my

dress.

"What's wrong with it, Mark? Why don't you like it?"

"Look at it." He blinks rapidly, and looks more than a little twitchy.

"I am. It's perfectly fine."

It's a gorgeous Roberto Cavalli, cherry red, low-cut silk halter, that narrows to my waist and then flares out. It dips low in the back, but it also has a slit up the leg that hits my thigh. It's absolutely killer.

"Fine? That dress is not fine. You have to change. That's all there is to it."

"Change? I can't change. You're acting like I'm wearing something geeky."

"That won't do at all. Wear something else." He twitches some more.

"Like what? A golf shirt?" I blow out a breath and chance another look at Gina, and I swear she's biting her lips. What the hell is going on?

"A golf shirt would be better than that," Mark huffs.

This is so stupid. We are arguing over my dress when all this time I thought he'd be over the moon about it. When taking in a view of the room, it's not difficult to notice that everyone's enjoying our little spat. Reaching out, I grab Mark's hand and pull him into our room. Then I shut the door behind us.

"What's going on?" He wants to know.

"I might ask you the same." In all honesty, my feelings are hurt. I've spent a small fortune on this gown, and I think I look pretty good, even if he doesn't. The least he could do is pretend.

He goes all spaz again, jerking his head around as though someone is poking him with a cattle prod.

"Dammit, I went to great lengths to surprise you with this dress. I thought you'd love it and maybe even drool a little. I mean, I thought I was going to be the belle of the ball, but you're making me feel more like Cinderella sweeping the hearth." And fuck my life if a tear doesn't roll down my cheek. This is so not happening. My arms fly in the air as I say, "See, now look what you've done."

"That's not it at all," he says, coming over and wiping at my tears.

"What's not it?"

"You've got this thing all wrong. I think you are undoubtedly the most beautiful woman I've ever seen in my life, and that dress is gorgeous, too. Just not on you."

Right as I'm getting ready to smile, he drops that last bit on me. "What? You don't think it looks good on *me*?" I can't believe he said that.

"No! I mean, yes!"

"You know what? I think maybe I should go to the gala by myself." As I begin to turn toward the door, his voice stops me.

"Not in that dress you aren't."

"What did you say?" I ask.

"The dress. You can't go in that." He shakes his head and holds out his hand, palm facing me. "It would appear I can't communicate well when you're wearing that thing." He fists his hands and frowns. "Like I said, you're the most beautiful ... even stunning. But I'm losing my coherency around you dressed like that, and I'm pretty fucking sure every other man will, too."

"So, you like the dress on me after all?"

"Riley, it was never a matter of liking the dress on you. You'd look perfect wearing a paper sack."

Three hard raps on the door alert us.

"Come on, you two. We're going to be late."

It's Ryder with a two-minute warning.

"Coming," I yell.

"You'd better not be," he yells back, laughing.

"Ha-ha, not funny. You need to go back to comedy school," I shout.

Mark pulls me into his chest. "I'm not sure how I'll stand having every guy in there checking you out."

"Yeah, but think of this. You're the only one who gets to taste the goods."

"I'd better be," he says, sounding jealous.

"You promise I look okay?" I ask. "You've totally thrown me for a loop."

"Eagle, you are magnificent. You're going to be the death of me tonight."

"I swear it'll be worth the wait. When we get back here, I'll make it up to you."

"If I'm not a dead man by then. You don't have a sweater or anything you can wear around here?" He points at my chest and around my back.

"No," I laugh, "and I'd look pretty stupid if I did."

"Jesus, I can almost see your tits."

"You can not."

"Come on, you two," Ryder calls again.

Leaning into Mark, I kiss him. "We'd better go." We link our hands and join the others, where we get all kinds of curious looks. From the way Gina inches her way toward me, I know she's going to try to wheedle some information out of me. But I'll not breathe a word of what was said until later. I'm pretty sure every word of Mark's dress distress will come tumbling out of my mouth after a few glasses of wine. And Gina will be cracking up with the information, too.

We take the elevator down to the second floor because the gala is being held in one of the ballrooms in the hotel. As soon as we exit, a dozen or more cameras flash in our faces. At first I'm of the belief it's for the charity. After all, my cousin, Fletcher, is attending, along with my twin brother. Their presence is enough to stir a hornet's nest of activity. Luckily, for the charity, it was Fletcher's bye week, and he was able to break away from his quarterback duties. The Make-A-Wish Foundation should be happy. He has written them a sizable check because of this event.

But that's not why the cameras are going off like fireworks. Fletcher and Ryder keep moving and I follow, but the reporters stop me. Then the questions begin. It's about the little incident with Justin and how horrible it must've been for me to find my former fiancé in the, um, mouth, of another woman. They aren't shy a bit about what they ask, and I nearly forget to act like the spurned ex-girlfriend.

"It was so shocking, particularly since he should have been setting a good example for the children," I say, leaning on Mark for support. "If my caddie here hadn't come looking for me, I'm not sure what I would've done." I fan my face for effect.

Another reporter steps forward and asks, "Miss Wilde, do you think there's a chance of you and Mr. Turner patching things up?"

Is he kidding? Like there ever was a Miss Wilde and Mr. Turner to begin with. But I continue my acting skills and say, "After what happened, and this isn't the first time I caught Justin in a compromising position, my answer is a huge no."

Not waiting for any more questions, I walk, my hand on Mark's arm as he escorts me into the ballroom. More camera lights flash as we enter the red carpet area.

"This is crazy," Mark comments.

"Yeah, it is, but it's for a good cause."

"Is it like this all the time?"

"Like what?" I ask.

"The cameras. The paparazzi?"

"If I'm at a tournament, yeah. But otherwise, no. Why?" His question worries me, and he's fidgeting again, which make me more than a little uncomfortable. "Hey, are you still hung up on this dress?"

"Huh?" he asks as he gawks around the room, and then back at me.

"My dress. Is it still making you twitchy?"

"The truth?"

Facing him, I say, "Nothing but it."

His eyes zero in on my cleavage, which, to be honest, would be rather difficult not to do. The V in the dress runs down nearly to my waist.

"When I look at you, I'm undone. But the thing is, I imagine that every man in here feels the same."

"Is that a bad thing, then?"

"Fuck, Riley. What do you think? I don't like every man undressing you with his eyes."

"I would imagine that most women are doing the same to you." Smiling, I add, "I wore this dress for you, so you would do exactly that. I wanted you to be squirming all night, and I have to say, my mission is accomplished. But, Mark, I didn't realize you were so cavemanish." My tongue pokes the inside of my cheek as I hold back a giggle. And that's exactly where he's gone—straight to the Stone Age.

"What? I'm not like that."

My brow arches at his ridiculous statement. The giggle I was holding back bursts out of my mouth as my eyes nearly spin like a top. "You are the most possessive alpha male I have ever dated."

"How can you possibly say that?" he asks. And he's truly shocked by what I've said.

"Look at you. You're standing there as if you want to cage me in with your arms. And your eyes are darting around the room almost daring anyone to look at me."

His jerky head movements tell me he's doing exactly what I described before his gaze lands on me. But his focus only stays on me momentarily before it skitters away to assess his opponents in the room.

"There you go again. Obsessing, analyzing, seeing who you're going to have to fight."

"I am no— "

Cutting him off, I say, "Don't you dare deny it, Mark James. You are the absolute worst, and you suck at hiding it." It's comical, really, seeing this usually cool and composed guy go all dominating and proprietorial over me. Come to think of it, now I understand why he didn't hang around when all the photos were being taken that day, after Justin showed up. Seems to me the old green monster was showing its face.

He has this cute little way of tilting his head and lifting the corner of his mouth as he thinks about what I said. Makes me want to plant my lips on his mouth. Too bad we're not alone.

"Okay, maybe you're a little right," he says, rubbing his chin.

"A little? Either I am or I'm not."

"I admit you do have a point. I can't help but feel protective of you."

This I love. "And?" I prod.

"All right. I want to bust in the teeth of everyone who is staring at you. And believe me, there are many."

"Really?"

"Riley! Stop it. You're goading me."

His black tuxedo jacket is open, so I slide my hand inside and squeeze his waist. "Yes, I am. I can't seem to help myself. I wanted so badly for you to have lusty thoughts of me in this dress tonight because ever since I put it on, I've had this really hot fantasy of us."

I watch his throat work as he swallows. "Fuck."

"Exactly. Me bent over, you behind, with this dress pulled up to my waist," I whisper.

"Jesus. Will you excuse me for a minute?" he asks, his brow sweaty.

"Yeah, sure. Where are you going?"

"Bathroom," he ekes out as he moves away from me.

Gina's voice over my shoulder makes me jump as she asks, "So? Did it do the trick like I said it would?"

A husky chuckle leaves my mouth. "I believe so. He had to rush off to the bathroom for a minute."

Gina throws back her head and a loud howl, resembling that of a wolf's, lets loose. "Calm it down, girl." I feel like I need to pat her on the head.

"I'll bet you he had to rub a quick one out."

"Shut up!" I glance around to make sure no one is in earshot.

"What the hell did you say to him?" Miss Nosy asks.

I play zipper lips and say, "Not saying a word."

She sticks her lower lip out so far I'm afraid everyone will trip over it. "That's so not fair. This was all my idea."

"Um, no. The dress was your idea. Everything else was mine."

166

Ryder shuffles up next to us and asks, "What are you two conspiring?"

"Nothing," I answer quickly. "We're all good here."

The emcee interrupts this conversation, thank God, and kicks off the gala by asking all the golfers to step to the front of the room for acknowledgment. Mark still hasn't returned, and I look around to see if he's on his way back, but I can't find him. I'm sure he'll freak when he comes back and sees me up there in my half-naked concoction. The idea makes me laugh.

Once we're all assembled, the emcee, who is one of the board members of the Make-A-Wish Foundation, rattles off all the statistics of the event from the number of attendees and players to the amount of money raised. It's an impressive sum, and the round of applause nearly cracks my eardrums. The clapping goes on and on. Cameras flash forever, and when it's finally over, I rejoin my group. Mark has finally returned, but his hands are fisted and he's not happy.

"You okay?" I ask.

"Better now. Promise me something. Next time we go to something like this, you get my input on the dress."

Laughing, I answer, "Oh, hell no. If you think I'd miss this, think again. This has been priceless."

He growls as he takes my hand and pulls me in the direction of the bar. But the bar is not our destination as we pass it by.

"Where are we going?" I ask.

He doesn't answer as he keeps walking. Finally, he

stops in front of a door and opens it. It's super dark inside, but he pushes me through and closes the door behind me. When he turns on the light, I find we are in a small storage closet that appears to be used for janitorial supplies.

"It's time to bring that fantasy to life. I can't be walking around this damn gala all night with a fucking boner that's about to pop through my damn pants. Enough of this teasing of yours. Now, bend the fuck over and pull up your dress."

MARK

I'd come close to swallowing my tongue when Riley walked out of our room earlier dressed for the gala. Despite the amount of fabric used on that dress, she's not wearing nearly enough to control the wolfish side of me that wants to mark her as mine.

Greedily, I help her lift fistfuls of her skirt out of my way. The only thing covering her tight pussy is a small scrap of something no bigger than my hand.

"Fuck, Riley," I gruffly say, as I free my cock from my pants.

Wickedly, she grins at me over her shoulder, knowing that she has me in knots over her choice of wardrobe or lack thereof.

"I thought you'd like that," she teases.

I bend to bite her shoulder before capturing her mouth with a soul-baring kiss. This woman, she's got me like no other.

Focusing on the task at hand, I probe her entrance with the head of my cock and find her wet and ready for me. I bite back a groan as I slide into her warmth, letting it envelop me.

She too is taken by all the sensations and moans so loudly, I have to cover her mouth with my hand.

"You're going to have to be quiet or I'll be forced to stop," I chide.

After she nods, I remove my hand and brace it on the wall as I begin to move inside of her. With my other hand, I slide it under her dress and find her braless. I should have guessed with her back exposed, but women have all kinds of things they wear for different solutions, I just assumed.

"Dammit, Riley, you like teasing me. But you won't think it's funny if I go to jail tonight for killing any asshole who dares to look at you."

She fucking giggles. I palm one of her perfect breasts and squeeze, which stops her laughter. Her neck stretches back as she moans.

"You like it when I lose control, don't you?" I murmur into her ear.

She nods and bends her head toward the floor, getting lost in pleasure.

"Yeah, well, I like you on your knees taking my cock deep in your throat."

Just picturing that has me tightening my fingers around the base of my cock so I don't nut off like a cannon. No woman has made me lose control like she does.

The angle isn't exactly right, and I have to use both

of my hands to spread her ass a little so I can slide deeper into her cunt.

Sounds of slapping flesh and her pussy squeezing me so tightly with each push inside her have me on the edge. I move my fingers to rub over that bundle of nerves. She lifts up on her toes as her sex milks the cum right out of me.

I bend down to bite at her lip over her shoulder before kissing her to mute the noise each of us makes.

My choice of location works, because I find a brand new roll of paper towels to clean both of us up before straightening her clothes and turning her to face me.

"The dress worked," she says, grinning at me.

"If you call this working."

I'd been called many things, a patient and gentle lover and a man who takes his time giving pleasure as much as he gives. But with her, I feel like an animal who acts only on instinct.

"I like when you go growly caveman. It's hot."

"Keep dressing like this, and we'll be the next headline after Justin. *Caddie Goes Wilde*."

She laughs. "You're not my caddie anymore."

It shouldn't bite, but it does. I liked being out there, helping her see the shots. We'd felt like a team, and she needed me. But knowing she's mine, tamps those feelings down.

"What am I?" I ask with a lopsided smile.

"Mine."

I couldn't have said it better myself.

Her hands reach up and fiddle with my tie and shirt collar before smoothing down the lapels of my jacket. Then she tucks her fingers under my waistband ostensibly to fix my shirt.

"You keep your hands there and we're moving on to round two." Her radiant smile has me swallowing. "Do you know how beautiful you are tonight?"

"With you looking at me that way, I feel it."

We should probably go, but I have to kiss her again. This time is slower as I savor the taste of her.

The rest of the party I play the gentleman making small talk as Riley works the room. So many people want her company as we are hardly given any time alone. She's stepped off to talk to a rep from Make-A-Wish as I watch, drinking her in. That's when my best friend comes over to stand with me.

"So, Riley," Fletcher says.

We've talked some, but he's been more than a little busy. And the last real conversation I had with him, I told him I'd fucked her and it was a one-time deal.

"Riley," I say, repeating her name before taking a sip of wine from my flute.

He claps my back. "It's about damn time."

"Time for what?"

"Time for you to settle down."

I nearly choke. "Fletch, we've just started this thing. I doubt she's even ready for marriage, and who's to say I am?"

"Uh huh, what about in high school over the summer

172

that one year and what happened between you two?"

"You knew?"

The kiss Riley and I had shared back then had been far too brief. And then she'd left to go back to California.

"Mom saw the two of you and asked me about it."

"What did you tell her?"

"That I didn't know shit." He laughs. "Not in those words. But you hadn't told me, though I thought you'd eventually say something."

"Well, it was only that once."

"And now?" he asks.

"And now I'm making up for lost time."

Later that night, I do just that. Steady are our nights. It's like after all the fast and rough, I have to prove to her that I can take it slow and easy.

The next day, the woman fawns over my godson. And Riley hears the news about standing up for her brother at his wedding. Then they talk dresses.

"I'm not wearing a tux unless Mark is wearing a dress," Riley says.

That gets a lot of laughs at my expense.

"I'm seriously considering making him wear a kilt," Gina says.

I groan, praying she's kidding as everyone laughs more. Then we watch our friends and family go, one by one. Everyone's going back to their lives. Even I have a moment to miss them for a second once we are alone.

As we get ready for dinner, I keep snatching glances to make sure Riley puts on something that won't leave me hard for the night.

"What?" she jokes, catching me glance at her.

"Just wondering if I need to go buy a cock ring."

She laughs. "You know that's used to keep your dick hard."

"I do. But it accomplishes that by keeping everything in. If I put it on before, maybe it will work by keeping everything out."

Walking over, she kisses my cheek. "Don't go to such drastic measures. I have plans for your dick tonight. I'll just wear pants, and maybe that will keep the big guy in check."

She winks at me before moving away.

"You could wear a garbage bag, and I'd get hard. I already have images of your gorgeous naked body in my head. And they won't go away."

As it is, she prances around the room in a black bra and a matching bottom that covers little. I have to turn away before I toss her onto the bed and fuck the shit out of her again.

"I promise to be on my best behavior."

But that isn't the case. At dinner, we sit and Ben shares with us the first time he met Samantha, his wife. I have to laugh at how they met in the produce department of a grocery store. The two of them trade back and forth effortlessly as they share each of their perspectives. When they talk about Samantha squeezing the fruit, Riley's hand lands on my lap and it's too late to stop her from squeezing and getting a rise out of me.

"How did you meet?" Samantha asks.

I cough because Riley has a death grip on my dick under the table as she strokes me through my pants.

"Oh," Riley says breathlessly and then giggles. "We've known each other for a while. Friends of the family. Let's just say I've wanted to get my hands on him since high school."

"And why didn't you?" Samantha questions.

My hand covers Riley's, and she smirks playfully at me before letting me go.

"Well, there was a girl and now that girl is going to marry my brother." Ben and Samantha look shocked, which is what Riley had been going for. "Anyway, back then my family lived across the country and then we lost touch."

Riley glances at me and bites her lip before springing another award-winning smile at me. She has no idea how that one look from her has me inwardly squirming.

"Sounds complicated," Ben jibes.

"Not exactly." I try to say, but my focus has already fled from the conversation to Riley. I take a second to regroup. "The girl, Gina, now a woman, is a friend and has always been one. Stupidly, as many teenagers do, we made mistakes. We tried to mix becoming more than what we were, and we quickly realized we were better as friends than anything else."

"It sounds like everything worked out. I have to say that for me, it wasn't until I had to work for someone did I truly appreciate the right woman," Ben says.

"Agreed." I think about the woman next to me.

We wait for dessert, and Riley's earlier torment will earn her fast and dirty tonight.

"Well, we should get down to business. At least my accountant will tell me if we don't talk business at all during dinner, I can't write it off."

Chuckling, I wonder what he has to offer.

"Dad and I want you here, but you know that." I nod. He hasn't been subtle about that from the beginning. "We are prepared to more than double what you were making before."

My brows rise.

"And," he adds. "You know we want you to come to Charleston for a test run. What we can do is offer you a conditional contract that removes the non-compete clause for a specific period of time. That will allow you to walk away with any clients you bring in if things don't work out before the trial period ends."

He pauses as I think it over. Being able to walk away with my clients and not have a non-compete agreement is tempting. If I don't have that, I would be unable to work anywhere without moving.

"It will give you time to see our processes and decide if we are a good fit. I'll be honest with you. We need you in order to set up a satellite office in Charlotte."

Riley's grin freezes. "How long will you need him in Charleston?" she asks.

"Just a few months," Ben says easily.

But I hear beyond her question. We don't talk for a

while after dessert and coffee arrive. Later at the hotel, after fast and dirty, we pack our bags to leave in the morning, Riley is subdued, a little too much so. She hadn't said much on the ride home.

When she breaks the silence, her question sounds casual. "Are you going to take it?"

I'd be crazy not to. "It's a solid offer."

"I know this is an amazing opportunity. But have you considered going at it on your own?"

Nodding, I say, "I have. There are a lot of risks. And working for Rhoades takes that away. I can eventually be independent for the most part without the gamble of going at it alone."

"So, you don't like taking risks?"

Where is this going? But I know better than to speak too quickly. Women tend to dance around the questions.

"I take risks," I say.

She nods and doesn't speak for a little longer. And I feel the need to fill in the silence.

"I'm not opposed to starting my own business. Hell, that's what Rhoades is bringing me in for. Starting up an office in Charlotte will mean using my ingenuity to get the business off the ground."

"Why not do it for yourself and not for someone else? Don't get me wrong. He seems like a great guy. I enjoyed dinner with both of them tonight. It's just…"

I know what she's about to say.

"It's just your job requires you to be independent. Everything rests on your shoulders, win or lose. And it's a risk, but you take it every day."

She tilts her head in agreement.

"True, it's doable. But I didn't grow up with money. What I have, I earned. If I gamble it and lose it all, where will I go? What? Will I have to beg to live with Fletcher or you when I'm homeless?"

"Don't you risk it every day when you play with the stock market?"

She's right, but I haven't had to live hand-to-mouth in a long while. I have no desire to go back to that struggle again.

Her phone chimes. She picks it up and has a conversation with someone on the other end. When she ends the call, I'm taken aback by what she has to say.

RILEY

For the first time, I dread the conversation I'm about to have with Mark. Even though he's supportive of my career, I have this sense of foreboding over what I am about to tell him.

"What was that call about?" he asks.

There's no use in delaying this. Plunging in, it's as though I'm diving headfirst into an icy pond. "I've just been invited to and accepted a spot in the Australian Invitational Christmas LPGA Open. It's being held in Sydney the second week in December. I would love for you to join me," I say with my hand on his arm.

His eyes change from curious to wounded and instantly droop at the corners, and my gut sags right along with them. "Riley, you know that's impossible. If I take that job Rhoades is offering, there is no way I can go to Australia, or anywhere right now, for that matter."

"But—"

"You heard what he said. I would be in Charleston

and then Charlotte, setting up the business. And you have to admit, it's an offer I can hardly refuse."

This isn't something that should surprise me, and I say as much. "But we can work through this, right? I mean, my job is going to take me away a lot, and I can't expect you to come with me at the drop of a hat. You have your career, and I have mine, right?" The questions pour out of me, and I'm making it sound so simple, when in fact, it's not simple at all. The idea of being on the other side of this gigantic world from him scares the shit out of me. Who am I trying to convince more, him or me?

"Come here." He grasps my hand and pulls me to the couch, where we both sit. "Yes, we can do this, and yes, we both know this was bound to happen sooner than later. But I'll be honest with you. I don't like it one single bit. I want my girl with me every day. And in my bed every night."

And don't I want the same thing? But what am I supposed to do? I can't only play in tournaments close to home.

"This is a tournament that I've been trying to get in for … well, ever since I made the LPGA. It's huge and an honor to be invited. They only invite the top players in the world. I couldn't turn it down."

"And I would never ask you to. I only wanted you to know how I feel."

"Do you think you'll ever be able to travel with me?"

His eyes never waver as he answers, "Honestly, I

don't know. Not for a while, I would assume, if I take the job. But then again, if things go well, who knows?"

There's no solution for this dilemma other than to live separately. I imagine other golfers have to live this way and so will I. The worst thing is, we've only arrived at the point in our relationship where I'm having seriously deep feelings for him and would rather not leave now. But it could have a huge negative impact on my career if I don't. Considering all the shit that just went down with Justin at this event, I need to show up with my happy game face on and let the world know that Riley Wilde is at her best.

"Wow. I never imagined this would be so hard."

He runs a hand over his already mussed up hair. "Neither did I," he says, his voice like sandpaper. "So, how long did you say you were going to be gone?"

"I didn't. I'll have to leave a week before since it's so far away, which means the week after Thanksgiving. The tournament is the second week in December, which means I won't finish until a week before Christmas." And then I get to the other part of the problem. "And I spend every Christmas in California with my parents, so it would make sense for me just to go there afterward."

His crestfallen expression brings tears to my eyes.

"That means we won't be spending the holidays together then."

"No, I suppose we won't." But then a thought hits me. I perk up and say, "Unless you want to meet me in California?"

His hand rubs at his mouth before he answers. "That would be unlikely since I would either still be in Charleston or in the middle of opening the Charlotte office by that time."

My heart pinches at his words. He's made his final choice. "So, you've decided then?"

"No. But think about it, Riley. With you on the road, I need something to do. And I also need an income. This opportunity takes care of both."

My conscience tells me to root for him and that this is a fabulous thing. So I do just that. "I think it's a fantastic option for you, Mark. You should take it, and if you do, I'm hoping you show Rhoades that you are worth every penny and then some. I know you are."

"He'll certainly get his money's worth."

"What do you mean?"

He lets out a rough laugh. "It's not like I'm going to have anything else to do."

Do I detect a bit of resentment?

"Are you angry with me?"

He doesn't respond immediately, and his eyes don't meet mine either. When they do, I search their bluish-gray depths. What I find is many things, but anger isn't any of them. Hurt and disappointment are, though.

"I would've expected a little more warning. That's all."

Taking his hand, I run my finger in a circle over the lines on his palm. "I would've given you one, if I had one. It was as big of a surprise for me, too. But you know something? I'm glad this happened, because this will be the first of many. And these situations are things we will always have to deal with. If we can't handle them, then we need to think about this relationship."

"Yes, you're right. We do."

Tied up in knots doesn't come near to how my stomach feels. It's more like tied up in barbed wired with a snake twisting through it. And I am probably going to feel this way until I get back to him from this trip.

"I have a suggestion."

"What's that?" he asks.

"Let's make the most of the next few days. We only have that many until my family comes for Thanksgiving and then you'll probably have to come back to Charleston for your training. That begins our separation, and quite frankly, I don't want to think about that right now."

He doesn't answer, but rather stands and walks to the sliding glass doors that lead to our little balcony. He opens them and moves through to the outside. It's a lovely night with the stars sparkling over the ocean and the moonlight lighting a path out to sea. Sliding my arms around him from behind, I expect him to put his hands on me, but he doesn't. He's as still as a stone pillar, and I'm not getting good vibes at the moment.

"Are you okay?" I ask.

"Yeah, just trying to work through this in my head. I'm sorry. The numbers guy in me has come out, and I can't seem to figure out a way around this. And it's annoying as hell." He spins around and tilts my chin with a finger. "I don't want to be away from you that long."

"It's not very high on my list either, Mark, but I don't see any solution. Neither of us can be in two places at the same time."

He puts his forehead against mine and says, "Then we make the best of what we got."

I tug on his hand until he follows me into the bedroom where he slowly undresses me. Our usually heated kisses are slow and soft, and he even lays me gently on the bed and gazes at me for the longest time. For the strangest reason, I get the feeling he is committing to memory everything about the night. Every single thing he does is carried out with purpose, carefully and methodically, as if he doesn't want to miss even the tiniest detail. It's in the way he kisses my neck, to the way he sucks my nipples, even the manner in which he licks my sex. His dirty talk all but vanishes as silence descends on the room. This is a new Mark, one that scares me to pieces. But I'm too far gone, too close to my release to say anything.

As my orgasm hits, he pushes inside me, and the dark intensity in his eyes is frightening. It's as though this is goodbye. And I don't know why.

When I feel him pour out his own climax inside me, he asks, "Why are you crying?"

My fingers touch the rim of my cheek and feel the dampness from my tear. "I didn't know I was," I say honestly. "But you're scaring me, Mark."

"Me? Why?"

"You're acting different."

His weight rests on one elbow, and ignoring my comment he says, "You're beautiful even when you cry. Did you know that?"

"No." And he's evading my statement.

"More beautiful than anything I've ever seen."

His mouth touches mine. "Your body is heaven to me. There's not a thing in the world about you I'd ever want to be different than how you are now."

What is he really saying? Is there something more? I decide to stay silent and let him speak.

"All those years passed, and whoever thought I'd end up with you?"

"I'd hoped."

"Not as much as I did."

I chuckle a bit. "Is this true confessions?"

"Call it what you will. I'm just making the best of things."

This moment, the way he looks at me, I want to blurt out, "I love you." But something—and I can't describe it—stops me from saying it. Maybe it's too new. Maybe it's the fact I'm leaving. I don't know. But his tenderness melts my heart further, and I am more aware than ever of the difficulty I will face when we will part ways.

Our idyllic stay at Kiawah ends, and we return to Charlotte for the Thanksgiving holiday. My parents arrive, and everything at home is topsy-turvy for the week they are here. Ryder and Gina are in the residence, and Mark is here as well. He comes in for the entire week, disappointing his family, only to make them happy with the news he'll be home for Christmas.

Mom is all eyes and ears when she finds out we are an item, as she calls us.

"So, Mark, tell me where you're working these days."

"Mom, you're always poking your nose into people's business," I say.

Mom points her eyes at me, and I instantly wither. She was always good at that.

"Riley, that was not a rude question," she snaps back.

"No, it wasn't, Mrs. Wilde. But as a matter of fact, I'm in the decision-making process on what to do." Mark explains the situation, and Mom listens. She advises him against Rhoades.

"You're a smart man. They obviously want you for a reason. Take what they want from you and run with it on your own," she says.

Hmm. I like that idea. But I see Mark's side, too. I'm off in la la land, dreaming of how Mark could travel with me, if only, when I hear, "Riley, what do you think?" Mom asks.

"Uh, sorry. What?"

She flaps her hand a couple of times, saying, "Never mind. Why don't you go and help Gina in the kitchen? God only knows if she can cook."

Mark lets out a laugh. "She's great with bar food. I'm not so sure about turkey and the rest."

Mom says, "I don't think your father will be excited about eating chicken fingers and fries for Thanksgiving."

"Jeez, Mom, I think we can figure out a turkey," I say, heading into the kitchen. At least I hope we can. To be perfectly honest, I haven't given it a thought, and I've never cooked one myself.

When I get in the kitchen, Ryder and Gina have this enormous bird laid out on the counter with a laptop next to it, looking up turkey recipes. Oh, shit. We are totally fucked.

"Hi, guys."

"Thank God. Do you know how to cook a turkey?" Gina asks, panic etching her features. The usual *I don't give a fuck* Gina is clearly rattled.

"Don't you just rub butter and shit under the skin and put it in the oven?" I ask.

Ryder looks at Gina and says, "We are clearly fucked. We should've ordered one."

"What does the Cooking Channel or whatever say?" I ask.

"You're supposed to brine it the day before," Gina says breathlessly, looking like she's about to cry.

A little mood lightening is called for, so I say, "Well, I suppose we can eat tomorrow." They give me a look that makes me want to take cover under the turkey roaster. "Okay, seriously, I was with a friend one year, and I swear all she did was stuff a ton of butter under the skin with a mixture of herbs and seasonings, and then basted the thing and it was delish. Oh, and she had one with a pop-out timer thingy, so she knew exactly when it was done so it wasn't overcooked."

Gina looks at Ryder, and he shrugs. "What do we have to lose?" he asks.

"Nothing but a turkey, a whole turkey, and that's the truth," Gina says.

My eyes twirl from their silly humor. At least Gina's halfway back to normal again.

"You all do that and I'll get the potatoes ready. Where are they?"

Gina yells over her shoulder, "In the fridge."

I open the refrigerator and can't find them. "Where?"

"See those four trays?" Gina asks.

My eyes scan the shelves, and then I see what she's referring to and I about faint. "Oh my God. Mom's gonna have a cow. You bought premade mashed potatoes for Thanksgiving?"

"Duh. Yeah, and gravy, too."

I nearly choke. "So, like, we're going to transfer these to a pan and hide these trays." I go to work on that. "If Mom comes in here and sees the potatoes done already, Gina, you're just gonna have to lie and say you fixed them yesterday or something."

"Or something," she says, her hands covered in butter. Then she grins wickedly and whispers something to Ryder and squiggles her fingers at him.

"Hey, stop it, you two. You are not alone," I warn them.

They laugh and finish prepping the turkey, stick it in the oven, and we work on the rest of the food items. When we've done as much as we can, we join Mom, Dad, and Mark. They're all laughing about something, and we soon find out it's a story about Ryder, Fletcher, and Mark from when they were kids and Fletcher got them all lost in the woods behind his parents' farmhouse.

"He bragged and bragged about how he could find his way around there blindfolded. And then it got dark, and we were huddled and freezing by the time his dad found us," Mark says.

Ryder jumps in the story saying, "Yeah, Fletcher always was directionally impaired. We'd go hiking, and he'd always want to take the wrong trail. Thank God for GPS."

When dinner is served, Mom wants to help in the kitchen, but we insist on doing everything. She finally relents and takes a seat at the dining room table. The turkey actually turns out to be pretty decent. Mom even says so, and Dad approves, too. The mashed potatoes, not so much. Mom ends up giving Gina all kinds of advice on how to make them the next time, while I have to bite my cheek to keep from laughing. Ryder kicks me under the table, and Mark squeezes my knee because I never had a chance to tell him.

Later that night, before we go to bed, in separate rooms at the beginning, I fill him in on the big potato joke. Then he tells me about how Mom's expectations weren't high to begin with. He leaves me at my door, but later in the night, I feel him slip into my bed.

"I can't let a night go by without you, knowing they're numbered," he whispers.

"I know. But Mom would die. The only reason Ryder and Gina get to sleep together is because Ryder is a guy and they're getting married."

"Ah, the old double standard," he says.

"Yep, and no fair."

"It's okay. Being here with you now, just having you in my arms, is plenty. Well, that's a lie. I want to be buried in you, but it'll have to wait."

Rolling over so I can see him, the light of the moon casts the room in a glow that's reflected in his eyes. He's so gorgeous, the way he stares. All I want to do is sink my fingers into his hair and bite on his lip.

"Mark, I..."

"What?"

"I'm going to miss you so very much." And that's not what I was going to say to him. Not even close. But I can't bring myself to say the words. I'm so damn scared.

"Me, too, Eagle. Promise me something, will you?"

"What's that?"

"You won't run off and forget about me. You know, absence makes the heart wander."

Is that a message he's sending me?

MARK

Chase, Fletcher's soccer playing brother, opens the door with his nephew in his arms.

"Merry Christmas and here you go," he says, passing him off to me.

It hurts to be reminded how many weeks it's been since I've seen or held Riley.

"Thanks." He starts to march off. "What gives?" I point to Harrison, my godson.

Turning back, he says, "Kids aren't my thing."

Fletcher mentioned that when he named me as godfather. He said his brother, at twenty-five, was not ready for kids yet. And what does that make me at nearly thirty? Gramps? Harrison coos while gnawing on something with a great amount of drool.

"How long are you in town?" I ask him.

He shrugs. "Through New Year's at least." He pauses, but then asks, "Where's Andi?"

I hadn't seen my little sister, who's six years younger

than me, for far too long. Mom couldn't have kids after me, and they adopted Andrea because she desperately wanted a daughter. I love her, but she's breaking Mom's heart lately. She'd gone to college in Chicago and hadn't looked back after graduating.

"I saw her last time you did. She hasn't been home since."

It's another reason I couldn't go to California to spend the holidays with Riley. My sister had given an excuse that as a neonatal nurse she works crazy hours, and it won't make sense for my parents to visit. It's the same reason she gave last year, too. I know she's hiding something, but my job has prevented me from checking up on her. Besides, she's been Miss Independent since she learned to walk. She never asks for help.

"Two years?"

"Two years," I agree. "You know how she is. She doesn't need anyone or anything."

"There he is. Hey, Mark," Cassie says, kissing my cheek before taking Harrison from me, and striding away. "You spoiled little man. If everyone keeps holding you, my job will be..."

She's gone before I can hear her finish that sentence.

"So, you and Riley?" Chase asks, before tipping a beer to his lips.

Cassie must have handed it to him, because he hadn't been holding it before.

"Yes, did Fletcher tell everyone?" I mutter.

"No, Mom mentioned it," he says, grinning.

Their parents are my second ones as mine are to them. Chase is younger than Fletcher by several years, but he still tried to hang with us until we went off to college.

"What about you?"

He glances away. "Let me go get you a beer."

I hear my mom and Fletcher in the kitchen discussing the menu. Fletcher and his dad can be heard in the living room with the game going. I stand there for a second, feeling like something is missing. It doesn't take long to know that besides the familiar voice of Gina and seeing my sister helping with the meal, I miss Riley.

The past few weeks have been hard without her, in more ways than one. In two different time zones, we haven't spoken very much except for a couple of sexy video chats. I've been crazy working as has she, just not confined to an office. Ben and the team have been great. And working there has opened my eyes to several things.

"Hey," Fletcher says.

I blink and realize I've been standing there in the middle of the living room, zoned out.

"You should go," he advises.

"What?'

"See Riley."

"I can't."

"Why not?"

"I have to be back in Charleston tomorrow."

"Don't make the mistake I did," he warns, yet again.

By the time I make it back to Asheville to call Riley,

she's wiped and we barely utter Merry Christmas to each other before she's begging off to get some rest.

Things feel off, and I'm hardly in Charleston for a couple of days before I'm back home for the weekend. By Saturday afternoon, I'm jonesing for her so bad, I search for flights to California. Riley should be back in town on Monday, but I can't wait a minute longer to see her.

My cleaning lady is going to kill me as I dump the contents of the suitcase I'd been using to travel onto the floor so I can repack. There's a flight that leaves in two hours. I don't buy the ticket because there is another in three in case I miss that one, but it's on a different airline.

A knock comes at the door. I've been expecting an overnight letter to be delivered from Rhoades. So I don't think when I open the door. It's then I lose the ability to breathe.

"Mark, are you going to let me in?"

"Riley," is all I can manage to say before I cup the back of her head and bring her lips to mine.

Whatever is in her hand falls to the floor as I kick the door shut. I've missed the hell out of this woman as I devour her mouth. She winds her legs around mine, and I move steadily to my bedroom. I shove the bag off my bed to clatter on the floor. I press her into the mattress, hard and ready.

"Take your clothes off, Eagle."

I stand straight and do the same, kicking my jeans off

somewhere into the pile. She's so damn gorgeous as she lies back and spreads herself for me. I lean down, taking one of her palm-sized breasts into my mouth. She moans, arching her neck back. Sinking inside her, I know for damn sure we've been apart for too long.

The whimpers that leave her mouth let me know she's feeling the same as I do. "Damn, Riley, I've missed you."

"Me, too," she breathes.

There are no more words as I pump inside her. I want to be gentle, but when her nails sink into my ass, my strokes become longer and quicker. I nip her shoulder at her neck as her nails rake up my back. She comes screaming my name. That's all it takes for my balls to draw up ready to fire. I pull out wanting to prolong things.

"On your and hands and knees," I command, slapping her ass before fisting my cock. A rosy handprint rises to the surface of her creamy skin, and I stroke myself a few times watching.

She gets into position, and I draw up behind her. Sliding my hand from her crease to her clit gets her back to bow. Cock in my hand, I aim it at my target and glide into her wet cunt. I bite off a curse and begin to move again. This time I keep one of my hands near her ass, probing at her puckered hole. My thumb breaches the barrier, and I mimic my in and out action while inching further inside.

"You haven't let anyone here?" I ask, briefly

remembering a conversation about this.

Her words are indiscernible, but the shake of her head isn't.

"Tonight I'm too fucking greedy, but I'm going to fuck every hole on your body before I'm done with you."

Taking out my thumb, I slide my index finger further into her. That's enough to send me careening over the edge to shoot off in rapid-fire precision.

It's not over. She's close to number two, so I flip her on her back and bury my face in her pussy. I get her off like the starving man I am. By the time I finish her off a third time and a second for myself, we're both spent. She curls into me as we finally both drift off to sleep.

When she stirs in my arms, I wake. Sunlight drifts in and warms my skin.

"Morning," she says with a radiant smile.

That one word makes me realize something. I don't want to wake up without this woman ever again. And it may be crazy. We've only been together for a short time. But I've known her forever. I've had time to watch her strength and inner beauty grow into the woman she is. She may have lived across the country, but I saw her every year since we first met as kids.

I'm about to confess that when she says, "Don't tell me you didn't decorate for Christmas. This is so sad."

Grinning, I tug her out of bed. Both of us walk naked into the kitchen where I point at the window ledge.

"See."

She laughs and walks over to the one foot Christmas

tree my sister sent me with a letter threatening me to put it up somewhere. It came decorated and had lights.

"Plug it in," I joke. "It lights up and everything."

She turns around, and I have a hard time not admiring her tight body.

"Did it come with wrapped presents, too?"

I lick my lips. "Not exactly. Those are for you."

She stares at me, and I know I broke one of our rules.

"But you said," she sputters. "Everyone agreed, no presents."

"You agreed. I went along with it. Besides, I just happened to come across it."

She picks up the baby blue box with its white ribbon and holds it up. "You just happened to be in a jewelry store?" she asks with one brow raised.

I shrug. "I have a mother and sister I had to shop for. When I saw this, I knew I had to get it for you." I indicate for her to open it.

Narrowed eyes land on me, promising I'll pay for it later. She tugs the ribbon, which falls open. When she removes the top, her eyes grow wide.

She lifts the delicate necklace and its charm. "It's gorgeous."

Her eyes are huge, and her lip trembles. I'm not sure if it's good or bad.

"So, you don't think it's corny?"

"No."

Her voice breaks a little, making me wary. Women are hard to read at times, so I hurry with an explanation.

"They swear that it's light enough to be worn every day, but sturdy enough to not break."

Tucking a finger under the golf club charm, she lets the light play over the attached jeweled golf ball.

"Please tell me it's crystal."

She's referring to the faceted diamond. I shake my head.

"You're crazy. This must have cost a fortune."

"Stop thinking about it. You're worth it. Let me put it on you."

Handing it over to me, she turns so I can stand behind her to fasten it around her neck.

When she spins around, the platinum and diamond necklace falls just below the hollow of her throat.

"You shouldn't have."

I touch it before sliding a finger between her breasts.

"You can make it up to me."

On her toes, she kisses me in a way that should have been the start of something. Only she slowly draws back.

"I have news," she says.

"I do, too. You first."

When her smile changes to something that resembles a brave front instead of great news, I remember something.

"Congratulations."

Her grin lifts a little. "Thanks. Actually, winning has opened some new doors." Her pause is an indication that what she has to tell me she's not sure I'll be happy about. "I've been invited to play in the Singapore Open."

Singapore is on the other side of the world. Still, I manage a grin. "Wow, that's great."

"It is."

When she glances away, I think I already know what she's going to say. "When is it?"

"A couple of weeks. I have to leave in a few days so I can acclimate myself to the time change and get some practice time in."

"Oh."

I wait for her to ask me to go with her, but she doesn't.

"You have news?" she asks.

So many thoughts play over in my head. There's much to say, but I opt instead for this.

"Yes, you didn't open your other present," I say, scrambling to shove the other words back.

I don't know if it's pride, but I don't tell her what I'd planned to. I don't want her to feel pressured or obligated for the conversation that will follow. I'll tell her when she returns.

Grabbing the other box, I hand it to her and ask, "When do you think you'll be back?"

"A couple of weeks unless something comes up. But I'll definitely be here in time for Ryder's wedding."

She just got in town, and she'll be gone again. *Get used to it*, I tell myself. *This is what you signed up for.*

"Go ahead and open it," I tell her.

She does. Under the wrapping paper, the brand on the long white box makes it easy enough for her to figure out what's inside.

"A watch?"

"I was getting one for myself when the guy showed me all the features. He said it could send my heartbeat, too. It sounds cheesy now that I say it out loud. I just thought … with you gone so often, it was a way for me to let you know I was thinking about you."

Her kiss is hot, and the box lands on the counter next to her ass as I hoist her up. I'm inside her without a thought, fitting us together like the last missing puzzle piece.

It's a feeling I hold on to hours later after she leaves, begging off that she has mounds of laundry to do and repacking. I could have gone, but my ego stops me. Again, she hasn't asked for my company, and I don't want to crowd her. Gina warned me not to early on. So I let her go and busy myself with getting work done. With the news she's leaving, I have to make the most of the time she's here, as she'll be gone again for another few weeks after that.

A few days later, she opens the door and jumps into my arms, and I have to say I'm prepared to forget everything. But as I set her down, it's not lust in her eyes, but worry.

"What's wrong?"

She shakes her head. "It's nothing."

"Riley," I warn.

"I've been blasted on social media."

"What?"

"Some zealous fan of Justin's thinks I'm the bitch from hell."

Anger vibrates through me because I can tell she's more than rattled.

"What did they say?"

"Just that I'm a slut who deserves no less than death for breaking Justin's heart." She waves it off as if I can forget the look in her eyes. "Apparently, Justin's trying to do damage control from getting caught with his pants down by citing how easily I've moved on from him." She rolls her eyes before walking away toward the kitchen. "Let's not talk about it. I need to finish getting ready."

"You should have called me. I don't like the idea you were alone to deal with it."

"I wasn't. Chase was here. Anyway, we're going to be late. I'll be ready in a few minutes."

She doesn't give me a chance to quiz her more. She dashes off as Chase walks into the room with a bag in his hand. I don't go all crazy on him because I trust them both.

"What's up, man?" he says, clasping my hand. "And don't worry. Your girl was upset, understandably, but it's your garden variety bullshit."

"She should have called me," I growl.

"And this is why she didn't. Trust me. She's okay. Just some Twitter posts. Nothing more."

Breathing doesn't totally calm me.

Chase ignores me.

"And don't think anything of it. She didn't call me. I

was already around. Ryder let me chill here because staying at my parents' house wasn't an option, and Fletcher has a tiny human alarm that goes off all hours of the night."

I don't correct him that it's technically Riley's place now because I'm glad someone was with her.

"You know how it is," he continues. "If I stay at a hotel, next thing you know, based on what Riley's dealing with, I'll be in a picture with a woman I only stood next to on an elevator, and I have enough shit to deal with."

I decide that I'll talk more to Riley about what happened and push my anger back.

"Where are you headed?" I ask him.

"To fix a mistake."

"Care to elaborate?"

Chase isn't exactly Chatty Cathy.

"I'm going to see a woman I never should have walked away from. Hearing about Cassie and Fletch, I don't know…"

But I do know. Cassie and Fletcher's relationship is somehow infecting everyone like a virus, including me. Who wouldn't want what they have when you see it in person? Hell, Gina caught it, and she's one I never thought would ever settle down.

"There aren't enough women in Italy for you?"

He runs a rough hand through his hair. "Yeah, there's one named Lucia. She was convenient. A woman I could take to events and let off some steam with. But you know how the press is." I do. "They made more of it than it was because she was always there. And one day she sets me up. Has me take her to a jewelers to get her necklace fixed." He huffs out a breath. "Next thing I know, it's in the papers we've gone ring shopping. A few days later, she's photographed with a suitcase going in my place. Headlines read we're living together. And don't you know, there's a lot of shit of hers there and I didn't know when that happened. Anyway, she starts talking about the future. That's when I know the wrong woman is in my bed."

"Damn." I can understand why he's been rather quiet the last few times I've seen him.

"Yeah, so take it from me. Don't let her go. Riley's hot and she's cool. Don't fuck it up like Fletcher and I did. Although he's got Cassie back, wish me luck that I can do the same."

We knock fists. "So you're flying out. Will she be surprised?"

"Actually, I haven't talked to her. I just found out where she's living, and I've chartered a flight. Chris, you know my buddy from school, he's booked me an Airbnb so no one will sell that info to the gossip sites. Besides, I have to know. I have to give this a shot and hope she'll come back to Italy with me."

"What about Lucia?"

"She should have all her shit moved out by now. She's not happy, but I cut her loose."

"And if this woman won't go with you?"

"My agent is quietly talking to some US teams."

Fletcher mentioned something about that to me. I didn't know it was over a woman.

"Your brother said any contract here won't be as lucrative as those in Europe."

"They won't. But what's the point to having a bunch of money if you don't have anyone to share it with? Trust me. It's lonely as fuck even with a beautiful woman in your bed. I have to know if this girl's the one, because it damn sure feels like it."

"Going to give me a clue as to her name?"

He shakes his head. "Not yet. I want her to be the first to know how I feel about her."

With his bag in his hand, he calls out a goodbye to Riley. When she walks out again, I'm at a loss for words. She fucking owns the air I breathe. And he's right about a lot of things. What's money, what's a job without the one woman by your side who completes you?

"Eagle, you're going to have to call and cancel our reservation."

Wickedly, she grins at me. "Why?"

"I'm eating in tonight."

RILEY

"Hmm. Eating in?" I laugh at Mark. His brows are drawn together, and his expression is as serious as I've ever seen. It must have to do with Chase leaving and the two of us being alone. Good thing he didn't change out of his jeans either.

"You got it. I'm not wasting a single minute with you when we can be alone here, just the two of us, doing things we can't do anywhere else. No way do I want to waste the little time we have together in public. There are all kinds of naughty things I want to do to you that can't be accomplished in the middle of a crowd."

Playing coy, I ask, "What exactly did you have in mind? Netflix? There's a new show I've been dying to watch."

"I'll give you a show that's much better than anything Netflix has to offer." His sly grin has me clenching my thighs.

"Is that a fact?"

"Indeed it is. And I'll take it a step further. I'll order in, and after the food arrives, we'll only have one rule."

Now he has piqued my curiosity. "And what's that?"

"No clothing allowed."

My pussy throbs, and I have to squeeze my legs together now. The clenching thing isn't cutting it anymore. My upper lip may be a little sweaty, too. Sex with him is like no other man before.

"Well?" He prompts my silence.

"Yeah, I'm in. Hurry and order." I don't add, *or else I might have to take a quick trip to the bathroom and get myself off right quick.*

A sexy chuckle comes from the kitchen, where he's gone to find the menus Ryder and I keep for takeout. "Hey, Riley, what drawer are they in again?"

"Under the coffee maker."

His hands are full when he comes back, but most of the menus are from pizza places, Ryder's favorite.

"Looks like sushi and Thai might be our best picks," I say.

Mark orders sushi, and the food arrives within a half hour. He eats as though he hasn't had a meal in days.

"Hungry much?" I ask.

Wiping his mouth with a paper napkin, he grins. "Sorry. I'm a little anxious to get you naked."

"Why didn't you just say so?" Setting my chopsticks down, I stand and grab my sweater by the hem and slowly pull it over my head. Next go the jeans. When I'm left in my lacy bra and thong, he stops me.

"No more. Finish eating. But wait. Can you do a little pirouette for me?"

Too bad I can't do the stripper dance. That would really get him going. Unfortunately, my rhythm is more of the pole and not the dancer. I twirl around on the balls of my bare feet, and he doesn't quite moan, but it's close.

"God, Riley, you're so fucking perfect, you hurt me."

He stops me in my motion to sit.

"Hurt you? How can I hurt you?"

"My balls are so damn blue, they're killing me. That's how." His hand is on his dick, and I can see it outlined, even through the jeans he's wearing. The slut in me wants to rub her hands together and pounce. Only I sit back down, very ladylike, and finish off my sushi roll.

"God, I love wasabi. I wonder..." My voice trails off.

"What?" He leans in and runs a finger down my neck to the hollow in my throat.

"Do you think it would heat up our, you know?"

"Your clit? Like fire?" His eyes twinkle with curiosity, much like mine.

"Yes!"

"I'm all for experimenting, but I think we should go easy," he suggests.

"Maybe we should try sriracha."

"Hmm. But then we'd have to clean it off. And they both might be a little sticky. I'm all for food porn, though."

Then an idea hits me. My knees wiggle, and I slap my

legs. "Oh, I have a better idea!" I'd purchased some of that tingling cream made for sexual stimulation a while ago. Gina told me about it, and I've had it upstairs, ready to spring it on Mark, but keep forgetting about it. Well, now's my chance, and I tell him about it, so I do.

"Whoa, there, Nelly. I'm not sure I want that tingle stuff on my dick. That might hurt or something."

Always the daredevil, I jump up and say, "I'll go first. I'll do it!" I was never one to back down from a challenge. "What's the worst thing that could happen? You may have to ice my pussy, and I'm all for that, too."

He squints as he looks at me, before waggling his brows. "I like that idea, too."

"I'm all in, Wall Street. Let me go get it." I run upstairs to my room and rifle through my drawers, looking for the stuff. When I find it, I tear back down the steps and crash land on Mark's lap.

"Excited much?" he asks, laughing.

"Oh, man, this is gonna be fun." I hold up the tube for him.

"Let me check the label just to make sure it's safe. I don't want to break your clit. I kind of like all your sexy parts as they are."

Elbowing him in the ribs, I say, "You are not going to break my clit or vag. It's all natural stuff, you big goof. Let's get our adventure on."

His smile immediately disappears. "You're not happy with our sex life?"

Oh, shit. I've hurt his feelings. Cupping his face, I say,

"I adore our sex life. When I'm away from you, all I want to do is hump the pillow in the bed. You're the only man I've ever wanted to get adventurous with, the only man I've ever trusted enough to do anything like this with."

The tube falls out of his hand as he wraps his arms around me, going in for the killer kiss. His tongue pushes its way into my mouth, and he thoroughly fucks it until I'm no longer thinking about a tingling clit. With my hand massaging the bulge in his jeans, I start to straddle him because I need some friction between my legs.

"What are you doing?"

"I want to climb on the Mark train."

"No, you don't. Not yet, anyway. Slip that off."

He points to my thong and grabs the tube while I do as he asks. Then he gets naked, too. "Riley, lose the bra while you're at it." When we both are free of clothing, he pats his lap, and I gladly climb aboard. "Now, let's have a little fun."

He only uses a tiny amount, but instead of rubbing it on my clit, he puts it on my nipples.

"Ohhhhh."

"Good? Bad? Tell me something here."

"I don't know. It's … it's … icy and hot!" And I giggle. Which sounds stupid to my ears.

"Yeah? Then how's this?" Now he dabs just a tiny bit on my clit.

"Holy shit!"

"Good?"

"Very," I pant as he rubs circles around me, then

slides a finger inside. The icy heat runs a trail from my clit down the seam that leads inside me. "This is unreal. You should try."

"Okay." He hands me the tube, and I put a tad on the end of his cock. I watch his face as it heats up.

"I need inside you. Like now."

Raising up, he inches inside of me, and the combination of the fire and ice it sends is intense. His thrusts are deep and hard, and his fingers tighten as he grabs my hips to direct the motion. My nipples still sting, and I reach down and pinch and roll them between my thumb and index finger.

"Fuck, that's sexy," he says. He plunges in hard and tilts his pelvis to drag his cock over my clit as he backs out. This action is repeated over and over until I scream out my orgasm, shooting off like never before.

"I want you from behind."

The burn is still strong, and I know I'll come again.

"Bend over the couch." I use the arm to support myself. "Yeah, perfect. What a gorgeous view. This ass is mine one day, Riley. You know that, right?"

"Yeah, just fuck me, Mark."

"No mood for talking, huh?" He chuckles.

He drags the tip of his penis up and down my slit and circles my heated clit not a few times, but a few dozen times. I'm begging, pleading, telling him I'll sell him my nephew, meaning Fletcher's kid, if he'll just stick his dick in me. When he does, it's slow. He teases me. One little inch in, and then out, then two in, then back out.

"You're torturing me. Stop," I say.

"It will be worth it."

He keeps it up until my nails have nearly bloodied my palms. "Pleeeaaase." My arm squiggles under my hips in order to reach my clit. If he won't do the job, I'm just going to get myself off.

"Get that hand out of there," he says.

"No, I need this. I ache."

"Riley." It's a warning. "If you don't stop, I'll quit and tie your hands to the bed so you can't reach yourself."

"You wouldn't," I challenge.

"Test me and find out."

When I don't move my hand, he picks me up and carries me upstairs to my room, dumps me onto the bed, and minutes later, I'm tied to the headboard with the sash of my robe and my thong.

"Mark, let me go."

He stands there, staring at me with a satisfied half-smile on his face. "Can't say I didn't warn you." Then he leaves. What the actual fuck?

He comes back upstairs with two glasses of water and a glass of ice.

"Let me go."

"When the time's right, I will." Then he digs in his bag a minute, but I can't see what for until he holds up a necktie and a T-shirt. A wicked grin appears on his sexy as hell face, which makes me squeeze my legs together. "You won't be doing that for long."

He grabs one ankle, and using the necktie, attaches it

to the footboard. I've already figured out he's going to use the T-shirt for the other ankle.

"Hmm. I may have to change your nickname from Eagle to Spread Eagle because you look damn stunning like this."

Licking my lips, I can't deny that I do feel sexy. Wetness pools in my core, and it's probably dripping out of me by now.

"Still icy hot in and out?" he asks.

"Not much."

He grabs the tube and applies a little. I suck in my breath as it hits. He also puts some on my nipples. It makes me writhe in my restraints, and about those— damn, it's fucking hot as hell being tied up.

When he slides in two fingers, I bite my lip, but moan. It's impossible not to. Even though he hasn't tied me tight, I can't move very much. I want to thrust to meet his fingers, but I don't.

"I want to feel you inside me," I say.

"Oh, you will."

Turning away, he gets something, only I can't see what. Then he releases my ankles and pushes my knees to my chest. His hand works me, my clit, vagina, but then I feel that same finger breach my backdoor, and at the same time, he pushes his cock inside me. I'm full, stretched to my limit, by him, his hand, and the icy sensation. I want to grab his hips, ass, anything, but I can't. He doesn't fuck me hard, but slow and steady, to a rhythm that is in perfect harmony with his finger, buried in me. They work together producing magic, and when I climax, I catapult off the edge in a magnificent eruption of impulses that don't seem to want to end.

Mark soon comes, and I feel his warmth against my icy depths. His pulsating cock takes its time, and when he's been choked dry, he lifts to one elbow and kisses me.

"You are amazing."

For the rest of the night, we have sex as many times and in as many places as we can think up. The kitchen counter seems to be one of our favorites. And the sink has a water sprayer. Who knew that thing would come in so handy and that Mark would come up with so many ideas on what to do with it? My ingenious lover. By the time the New Year's ball drops, we are bone weary from fucking, and we laugh as we clink our champagne flutes together.

"To the best New Year's Eve I've ever spent, and may this coming year be our best ever," he toasts. We raise our glasses one more time, and I'm instantly saddened over the prospect of having to leave him so soon.

How will we work this out between us? How can we keep this up? Will he even be willing to do it? I know one thing. I have fallen, and fallen hard for this man. If he isn't willing, I hope he tells me soon, because my heart is so wrapped up in him, even if he told me now, there isn't enough Gorilla Glue in the world to piece it back together.

RILEY

The tearful goodbye as he reminds me for the umpteenth time that my plane is going to be late has me questioning repeatedly why I don't ask him to join me. When I disengage myself from him, he grabs my chin and says, "We can do this, Eagle." Then his fingertips gently swab my tears away.

My head vibrates up and down, and I unsuccessfully convince myself he's right. The problem isn't that we *can*. It's that I don't *want* to. Sniffling, I say, "Pretty sure I look a mess."

"You never look a mess."

He's only trying to make me feel better, but it's not working. It's when he stuffs a handful of tissues in my hand, I know I must look like road kill. When I attempt to laugh and a snot bubble emerges from my nose, the situation turns a bit humorous.

"Look at me," he says. Grabbing one of the tissues, he wipes my nose, and I feel like a little kid. "There.

Much better. Now, you really need to be going, or you will miss that plane." He plants a loud smacking kiss on my lips and gets out of the car to assist me.

Pulling out all my shit is no small feat. Golf clubs and three large bags would break anyone's back.

"How do you travel like this, alone?" he asks.

"I hire a skycap at the airport. Usually I take a cab."

We drag my stuff to the curbside check-in, and then it's the final goodbye.

"Hit 'em well, Eagle."

"I'll do my best."

"Promise me something?" he asks.

"Sure."

"Text me when you land in Atlanta, Tokyo, and then in Singapore."

"You know I will."

Warm arms cage me into his body, and I don't want him to leave. Like I *really don't want him to leave. Say something, Riley. Just say it!*

"I'd better get going. Work, you know."

And those three words stop me. "Yeah. Work. Okay, I'll talk with you soon. I'll miss you."

"Me, too." He turns and walks to his car. My eyes are pasted to his back and remain fixed on him until he drives away.

"Ma'am, did you want to check your bags?" The skycap brings me back to the present.

"Oh, yes."

He checks me in, and I'm off to my gate. I board the

flight, and my ass is kicked—by me—so many times the damn thing is bruised. It's one of those *I shoulda, woulda, coulda*. But dammit, I didn't. And the thing is, golf is my life. It has been ever since my dad stuck a club in my hands and taught me how to swing. It wasn't a matter of telling me I had to practice. I begged to practice more. They had to drag me off the range and the course. This is the first time in my life I wish I had a different career. I'm that silly college girl whose boyfriend is attending a different school, and I'm pining away for him.

When the flight attendant comes by, I order a screwdriver. The flight from Charlotte to Atlanta is short, not even an hour. Maybe the vodka will relax me enough to take my mind off the long flight ahead. From Atlanta to Singapore it's over twenty-two hours, and I don't want to constantly think about this situation that long.

We land in Atlanta and not only do I text Mark, but I call him as I walk to the international terminal. Atlanta is crazy with all the subterranean trains and concourses, so I made sure I had enough time when I made my reservations.

"That was quick," he says.

"Yeah. The air traffic wasn't backed up like it usually is."

"You okay?"

"Um, I'll survive."

"I hope so. I'd like to think I'll see you again." There's not even the slightest hint of humor in his voice.

"You will."

"Hey, you're going to have an awesome tournament. In fact, I'm going to make a prediction that you'll win."

"Ah, Mr. Hopeful, are you?"

"No, I've seen you play, Eagle. I know the talent that lies in your swing. And I've also been the, um, recipient of the power of those hips."

The corners of my mouth curve into a smile. "Yes, you have, haven't you?"

"And I will again, in the not too distant future."

"Hey, I'm getting ready to get on one of those trains, so I'm gonna lose you."

"Okay. We can talk later. Be safe, Eagle."

My phone goes dead at that point, leaving me to muse over what I should've asked him again. Enough with beating myself up over this. I didn't ask and that's that. I plop onto a seat at my gate, and I'm surprised I can see my legs with the way my lower lip sticks out.

The call goes out to board my flight, and Mark seems further away than ever. This melancholy mood stays with me even after I step out of the airport in beautiful Sentosa and arrive at my gorgeous hotel. And why? Because I'm thinking of how much more meaningful it would be if Mark were here. The joy has seeped out of my life without him by my side. It all sounds so childish when I think about it, but it's precisely the way I feel. Too bad Wade couldn't fly with me, but he lives on the West Coast and that didn't make sense. Randy took a different flight, and I honestly didn't want him to see me moping over the fact that I left Mark behind.

When the tournament week arrives, I'm not playing as I should. Randy and Wade keep asking me what my problem is. Randy finally blames Mark, and he's right this time. But I deny it.

"Look at you. How much sleep are you getting?" Randy asks.

"Plenty."

"My rear end. Your eyes look like you're growing eggplants beneath them. Don't they, Wade?"

Wade shrugs, and I can't blame him for not wanting to get in the middle. But he does add, "You do look exhausted, Riley. Is it the time change?" he asks gently.

He knows perfectly well I'm a mess, too.

Randy grabs a club and inspects it. "Isn't this what I warned you about? Isn't this what I said would happen? Get involved with someone and you're bound to get hurt. Did he dump you?"

Jesus. "No, he didn't dump me, and he has a name. Please use it."

"Okay. Mark, then. So, what's the problem?"

"The truth?" I decide not to hide it anymore because it's no use.

"Yeah," Randy says softly, his eyes matching his tone.

"I know you'll make fun of me or something, but I miss him. We're so far away, and with this time change it's so hard to stay in touch. And I know you don't like him, so go ahead and beat me up."

I'm surprised when his burly arms wrap around me and hug me like my dad would.

"Hey, I get it. I miss my family, too."

Wade joins in, saying, "Oh, man, so do I. I'd give anything for my family to be here. This place is so awesome. My wife would go crazy, and that's all I can think about."

"How do you get through these times?" I ask. I need to know these things because this will be my life.

"You think about what waits for you when you get home. And it makes it all worth it in the end," Wade says.

"And then some," Randy adds. "You'll get through this. You're one tough cookie, Riley. This is the first time you've ever been in love so—"

"Who said anything about being in love?" I ask.

They both look at me and chuckle. But then it turns into an all-out howl session.

"Oh, come on. Stop kidding yourself. You've got it so bad for him, if it's not love, I don't know what it is," Randy says. "I've known you ever since you were in high school. I've watched you since before then, really. This is the one, Riley. Look, you know how I feel about this, but it was bound to happen one day. I just want the man who holds your heart to be of high standards. But I trust your judgment here."

This is something coming from Randy. I'm glad to see his pit bull attitude toward me relaxing somewhat.

Wade shuffles his feet, and his gaze shifts between

the two of us. I put him out of his misery. "Spit it out, Wade."

"I have to agree with Randy, although I haven't known you for very long. Whenever you talk about Mark, you sure get all soft. It's the way my wife acts around me. And don't be mad at me. That's a compliment. You know how crazy I am about my wife."

"Thanks." And he is crazy in love with her. He does all kinds of nice things for her when he's away, like sends her flowers and gifts from wherever he is, buys her jewelry, and even beautiful photos so she doesn't feel left out. He's an awesome husband.

Thinking about those things, my hand automatically reaches for the necklace Mark gave me, and I finger the charm and diamond golf ball.

"Like that bling you're wearing. Bet I know where it came from," Randy says.

That actually gets a grin out of me. "And you'd be right."

Randy claps his hands together. "So, now that we have this settled, shall we play some golf?"

"Yeah, I think we should." They've made me feel better on one hand, but on the other, I realize one glaring thing. I'm in love. Deeply, madly, passionately with Mark James. And what the hell am I going to do about it?

For one, get my game head back on. And I do that. But only after I film a damn hot video of me getting myself off. This twelve-hour time change between us makes sexy phone time difficult, as it was when I was in Australia. When I finally come, moaning out his name, I text him the thing with a message saying not to view it in front of anyone. He'll know exactly why. I end the message with: *I miss you more than I love playing golf. R*

That should clue him in to my emotional status where he's concerned.

Without Randy and Wade, I'm not one hundred percent sure I would make it through this thing. But their unending support and encouragement, and the way they boost my spirits, especially at the end of the day when I'm weary as hell, keep me going strong. In the end, I come in at the top of the leaderboard and win the tournament.

We sit around, celebrating at dinner that night, when his call comes in.

"Congratulations, Eagle. I knew you would do it."

"It would've been a whole hell of a lot easier if you had been here."

"Oh, yeah?"

"Oh, yeah. And if you don't believe me, then ask Randy and Wade. They had to listen to me moan and groan about how much I miss you."

"Um, Eagle, don't even talk about moaning and groaning. That video. Uh, yeah. Thank God you warned me. If I had opened that thing in front of anyone, it could've been a major embarrassment."

I laugh so loud, Randy and Wade want to know what's so funny.

"Is that Randy and Wade?" Mark asks.

"Yeah, we're out celebrating my win."

"Then I'll let you go. Call me when you get in."

"I will."

As we're eating, my phone rings again.

Randy laughs. "You're Miss Popularity tonight, and it's well-deserved."

Chuckling, I answer, thinking it's either Ryder or my parents.

"Hiya."

"Miss Wilde?"

"Yes."

"Hi, this is Ron Thompson. I'm the tournament director for the LPGA Hawaii Invitational. I know this wasn't on your schedule or probably not even on your radar, and it's late notice, but we've had an opening. I'm pretty sure we're not even up to your normal standards, but we would sure love to have you come and play in two weeks. Would that interest you at all?"

"Oh, I—"

"The purse is unusually huge for a women's tournament. Does that persuade you any?"

"Can you hold on a second? My caddie and coach are right here and I'd like to confer with them."

"Absolutely."

Shit. I want to see Mark, but this represents money for Wade and Randy as well. I have to think of others beside myself. I explain to them the situation.

"We're already here. We might as well go for it,"

Wade says. Randy nods his approval.

Getting back on the phone, I tell Ron Thompson we're a go.

"Excellent. I'll send you everything you need. And thanks. I think you'll enjoy this one."

My heart sinks. Now what am I going to do?

We finish dinner and go back to the hotel. There are travel arrangements to be made and a host of other things.

"Do you all want to take a couple of days here, or would you rather go straight to Hawaii and relax?" I ask.

They both want to jump on the Hawaii train. I email my travel agent so she can get all the reservations started. Then I stare at my phone. The dreaded phone call awaits. Golf has once again become my enemy.

I touch his name and wait for the phone to ring.

When I hear his voice, tears trickle down my cheeks. How am I going to survive this kind of life? My heart is already breaking, and we've only just begun.

MARK

The phone feels like a meteor in my hand, alien and radioactive. Staring at it doesn't change the short conversation I had with Riley.

Her words shouldn't have affected me the way they did. It's only another couple of weeks apart. I am man enough to handle that. Yet, it feels like a lifetime. Still, I try to power through without waking to her scent in the morning, the way she makes me laugh and challenges me to keep me on my toes.

For a solid week and a few days, I've labored on. But enough is enough. My ego has flown out the window. I have to see her, and today. My laptop hasn't seen such furious finger tapping as I search like a madman for a flight, which turns out impossible. The best thing I can find has three connections. I even try Fletcher, but Cassie is using the plane. So I call up my other ace.

"Gina, Love."

Her snicker comes through loud and clear. "I'm Love

now? You don't ever call me that, and you've never asked for anything. First time for everything. What do you need?"

"You wound me. You know I love you."

"Yeah, keep pouring on the love and the twins are going to get the wrong idea," she teases.

Ryder has shown his displeasure once when he made the wrong assumption about Gina and me.

"Tell Ryder to keep his panties on. You know you're my favorite sister but not sister."

"Uh huh. Ryder's coming back and I won't be able to talk, so spit it out."

"Okay, and I really don't want to hear about that." I push my fingers through my hair, not sure how to ask. "Look, I need a huge favor, and you know I wouldn't normally ask."

"Oh my God, Mark. I know you don't, which is why you should ask away because I owe you big for all the shit you've done for me over the years."

I rub a hand across the base of my skull.

"Okay, the thing is … I need to see Riley."

"Shocker," she adds sarcastically.

"I can't find a flight out today and—"

"Don't say another word. I'll call my pilot and get you there."

"Gina—"

"It's not a problem."

"I'll pay for the fuel," I interject.

It will cost five figures at least, but fuck it. I need my

girl now.

"You will do no such thing. I have more money than God these days, and Ryder's got that nine-figure contract. We don't need you to repay us. Besides, I have to pay the pilot to be on standby based on the contracts I inherited. You'll be doing me a favor by using the plane so my money is not being wasted. Plus, Ryder says that his sister has sounded miserable the last few days. I imagine it's being away from you that's got her down."

I don't know what to say because I'm hung up on Riley's unhappiness.

"Thank you, Gina," I manage.

"Don't thank me. Go get your girl. And tell her how you feel."

"What?"

"You're not fooling anyone. You are *so* in love with her."

After the call ends, the phone hasn't lost its foreign quality. Am I in love with Riley?

Shoving shit into a bag, I think about how I'd been ready to give Gina what amounts to the price of an average car to get to Hawaii today in order to see Riley. Does that spell love?

Next, I get a car service to take me to the private airport because I don't want to leave my car there. The jet is ready and waiting with white glove service when I arrive.

Thank goodness, Gina hasn't been distracted by Ryder. She does me another solid by sending me Riley's schedule and hotel information. Something I hadn't thought of with my one-track mindedness about getting there.

There's wifi on the plane, so the next few hours I wrap up some work, prepared to spend all my time with my girl when I arrive.

Gina also thought ahead when my addled brain could only focus on seeing Riley again. She arranged transportation to the hotel after I landed. It's early evening on a warm night, and I hope Riley will be in her room when I knock on the door.

For a few moments, there's only silence. I start to ponder my next move when I hear footsteps.

The door opens, and Riley stands there in a silky robe.

"Is that how you answer the door these days?" I half-tease and half-scowl.

She's sexy as fuck, but the idea some other guy could have gotten an eye full stirs the caveman in me.

"It is when you're naked, tired, and starving, waiting on room service," she replies.

"Hmm." I reach out and finger the robe. "How does your boyfriend feel about you opening the door dressed like that?"

She shrugs and then eyes me seductively up and down. "He's not the jealous type. Besides, he's not here."

When she bites at the corner of her mouth trying to suppress a laugh, I worry at the strength of my fly on the jeans I'm wearing. Fucking hell, she's beautiful and sexy and everything to me. I'm so sure of that now if I wasn't already while on the long flight here.

"Do you think he'd mind if you let me in?"

Her hair tumbles over her shoulders as she silently says yes. "I don't think he'd like that very much."

"Sounds like quite the guy if you won't even give me a chance to make it worth your while."

"He is. He's the tall, dark, and handsome type. You know, super sexy and extremely smart, especially when he's flown all the way out here to surprise me."

I step in, and with two fingers under her chin, angle her head so I can show her exactly what we've missed over the last few weeks.

Like a tango dance, we move inside. The door closes behind us, and I let my bag fall so I can use both of my hands to get her naked.

"God, I missed you," she whimpers, jumping up and winding her bare legs around me.

"Where's the bed?" I growl.

She points as her mouth fuses to mine. I follow her outstretched finger through a door and toss her onto the thing. I don't waste time getting my shirt and jeans gone.

"Commando?" she asks with a salacious grin on her face.

"I was tired, starving, and waiting for you," I say, playing off her words from earlier.

Pouncing, I'm inside her faster than she can gasp out my name. And damn, if one word doesn't come to mind.

Home. It fills my head as I bring us as close as two people can be, moving in tandem, creating delicious friction that will carry us both over the edge.

With her, time has no end or no beginning when we're together. The four-letter word I'd feared for so long doesn't even seem to encompass the feeling that swells in my heart.

When we run off that cliff together in an orgasm so hard we both shake, it's more than earth-shattering. It's eye-opening.

It takes moments, seconds, hours for us to get our breathing under control.

"You can surprise me anytime you want," she murmurs the words while she pants.

"Anytime."

There's so much to say, but I just stare and memorize her face. It's as if I'm seeing her for the first time. She bites her lip again, glancing away, acting shyly beneath my scrutiny.

"I probably look a mess."

Her hand comes up to push at hair so sexy, my dick will be on alert in moments if she keeps it up.

"If messes are stunningly gorgeous," I say.

Her face goes all pink, and damn, if she isn't a picture.

"I was about to shower," she says, scooting toward the edge of the bed.

"Sounds like I am, too."

I manage to grab her ass before she gets to her feet,

and my touch elicits a squeal from her. Our shower is long and playful. By the time we're done, we split her now cool meal that was left on the table just inside the door.

"Do you think they heard us?" she asks between bites.

"Eagle, I couldn't care less what they heard. I'm sure they've heard far more before."

At some point that night, I have to let her sleep. Tomorrow is the first day of the tournament. It's a struggle to let her up and out of my arms. The cool sheets are nothing compared to her body next to mine. I don't shower with her because I know I'll be a distraction. And this isn't a game. This is her livelihood.

Later after a quick breakfast, I stand next to Randy, who scowls when he sees me walk up with her. Wisely, he makes no comment, at least in front of Riley. Now she's at the first tee, and we watch her make the perfect shot to land beautifully in the middle of the fairway.

"So, you came," he finally says.

It's not a question. And I wait for his disparaging comments that are sure to follow.

"I did," I reply.

"I'll be honest. Seeing Riley so distracted these last few weeks had me on the edge of declaring I told you so to her about you."

I'm about to say something when he holds up a hand.

"But, you showed when it mattered most. She may

have pulled out the last win, but with her state of mind, I didn't see how she'd win this one. And I'm man enough to admit when I'm wrong. She might not have told me, but this old man knows she loves you and you her. And you're good for her. I approve."

He holds out a hand, and for a second I just stare. Then I take it and firmly shake his. The rest of the tournament is like we're old friends. I forgive him because I know he truly cares about her. No need to hold petty grudges. He didn't ever come between us because Riley has her own mind.

By Sunday, my girl is on fire. At the eighteenth hole, we wait for Riley to take her final shot.

As we do, Randy says to me, "You're familiar with the foursome event during the Ryder Cup?"

The Ryder Cup, being a tournament nothing to do with her brother, but a biennial men's golf competition between teams from Europe versus the United States.

"Yes, I am."

On the first two days of the tournament, there are four four-ball matches and four foursome matches each day.

Foursomes feature two opposing pairs, each with a single ball they take turns to hit. The team with the fewest strokes wins that hole. In the four-ball matches, each player has his own ball in play, but still plays on teams.

On the last day, there are twelve single matches, where all team members are required to play.

He nods. "They are mixing it up this off year and trying out a new event of mixed pairs, meaning a male and female golfer pairing up against another duo for a tourney in New Zealand."

"Oh, I haven't heard about it."

"It hasn't gotten a lot of press until the organizers got more sponsorships to offer a purse no one can refuse. Several of the top golfers joined in recently."

"That should be interesting."

"It should and," he rattles off the name of the number one golfer, "after seeing Riley win the last few events wants her for a partner."

Turning, I stare at him. "She didn't mention it to me."

I hate that it bugs me that he knows more about her life than I do.

"Of course she didn't. It's in a few weeks, right before her brother's wedding. She said she wasn't going because she wanted to spend time with you."

His words burn a hole in my gut, but we say nothing more as Riley steps up to her ball and the crowd is urged to be quiet. She started this hole with a three-stroke lead, so she would have to really fuck this shot up in order to lose. She's on the edge of the green, which makes the putt long. But she only has to get it close for a birdie. Concentrating for a few seconds, she finally taps the ball with precision. I hold my breath and so does the crowd as her ball heads directly for the hole. It slows and even if it stops a foot short, it will be a beautiful shot.

The ball continues to crawl a little further and a little more, defying the laws of science. When it sinks into the hole, the roar from the crowd, including myself, isn't surprising. What is, is Randy and I hugging each other while pumping our fists.

"That's my Eagle," I say, more to myself because she just eagled the hole, making the shot two fewer strokes than expected.

But it's when her eyes glance about until she finds me out of the crowd that I'm more than star-struck, more than a fan. I'm in awe of this woman, and I struggle with just how to tell her and not frighten her away. Having never felt quite like this before, I'm not sure of the rules.

The sun is still high enough in the sky when the trophy presentation happens. Riley is brought out in front of the crowd and press as speeches are said and the staggering seven figure winning payoff is announced.

It's still light out after she changes, so we could eat dinner in the clubhouse. At the bar, she can hardly keep still.

"We can go somewhere else if you want. You look like you have energy to burn," I say.

"Actually, I'm not very hungry."

She stares off in the distance where Wade stands with his family.

"That was nice of you to fly his family out for the weekend."

But then, Riley has a charitable heart and a loving

spirit.

Nodding, she says, "I felt bad that I'd kept him away from them so long. I know the feeling."

Her eyes are like stardust and twinkle up at me during her confession.

"Is that why you turned down the New Zealand tournament? For me?"

Her tongue darts out and slowly licks her lip. She doesn't mean for it to be sexy. It's a precursor for her biting her lip, but damn, if I'm not hard in seconds.

"So, Randy told you?" I nod. She tries to sound casual when she adds, "I've been thinking there will be a lot more tournaments."

"Not like this one."

"You want me to go?"

"I want you, Riley. But I don't want you missing out because of me."

"Well, I'm not going."

Her lip pokes out stubbornly as she lifts her chin. I want to kiss her in this moment, but I refrain.

"Okay, play me for it."

That stops her. "What?"

"You heard me. Play me for it. The person who wins the first three holes gets to decide if you play in that tournament or not."

She pats my shoulder indulgently. "We both know I'll beat you, so what's the point?"

"Maybe, but you're in a dress, you've just played eighteen holes, and I'm a guy."

I don't mean anything sexist about the last part. I only say it to goad her into my game because I know she can beat me and many professional male golfers.

"You think so?"

And there's my competitive girl as she stands straight and crosses her arms over her chest.

I lift my shoulders. "Go get your clubs and meet me outside."

Challenge issued. The question is, will she accept?

"Fine, but if we are going to do this, I want something more than I was already going to get, because I will win."

"What's that?"

I'm more than curious what she's going to offer to sweeten the deal.

"We're not just playing golf. It will be strip golf. I want you to walk back to the clubhouse naked."

I throw my head back and laugh straight from my belly. Only my girl would dare me to strip golf. But now, the game is on. I have to win because I won't be the one not wearing clothes.

"Never going to happen, sweetheart. You're the one in a dress and heels. And I know for a fact you didn't wear a bra."

"We'll see, hotshot. Meet you out back in five."

She saunters off, and I wonder if my plan will backfire on me. The first hole is a par 4, and it's not a tough one. I have to win it, or I will have to explain myself to security when we make it back because the next two are tough having watched her play them earlier. Still, I head off to the pro shop, which is closing. I coax the salesperson into selling me the only pair of gloves that will fit my large hands. They're white, but I'm going to need them. He looks at me like I'm a nut, but I figure if this is strip and I lose, I'll have one more item to take off.

When I meet her, she's got a cart and everything. No one is on the course. It's closed for the night, but that hasn't stopped us before. I keep glancing around to make sure we aren't followed as we head off. And we haven't been when we stop at the first hole.

"Those are my clubs you're using. Their length, weight, angle, shaft, and grip have been custom made for me. You are so going to lose."

"Ladies first," I say.

Granting me evil eyes, she doesn't argue. And I'm right. Her balance is off in heels, and her ball ends up just to the right of the fairway in the grass.

Smirking, I set up my tee. There is a reason why quiet is mandatory when a player is about to make a shot.

I'm in the middle of the swing when she blurts, "I'm not wearing panties either."

I shank the ball so bad in the dwindling light I can't tell where the damn thing went.

When I turn to glare at her, she smiles sweetly at me. "I know how you like to have sex in public, and I wanted to be prepared."

Pointing at my chest, I say, "Me? I think that's you,

Eagle, who has a fetish for public indecency."

"Public indecency?" With nothing in her hand, she slowly lifts the bottom of her dress to show me her bare pussy. "Do you call this indecent?"

Swallowing a phantom lump in my throat, I'm barely able to utter, "That's not fair."

"We set no rules. But if you want to be a baby about it, go ahead and take another shot."

I can't afford to lose this hole, so I take my mulligan like a man and hit a great shot. My ball lands perfectly on the fairway. In the end, I win the hole. I wait patiently for her to take off that dress. Only she takes off her shoes. Not only am I disappointed I don't get to admire her breasts, wearing the heels had been a disadvantage for her.

"Thanks," she says smartly as she discards them into the cart. "My next tee off should be perfect."

And it is. The second hole is disastrous for me. I concede and take off my shoes.

"I should have taken one off at a time," I mutter at the third hole when my ball stops at the lip of the hole and doesn't fall in. I have to lose my shirt.

"That was close," she says, grinning like she has nine lives. She slips a finger under my waistband. "Looking good." I want to hike her up on the seat of the cart and have my way with her. "I have to give it to you. You're pretty good."

"I'm good at a lot of things," I say, kissing her and holding back from fucking her on the green. Too soon we cart off to hole number four.

She bends over and wiggles her ass. When she stands, she blows me a kiss.

"Say goodbye to your pants and a win because I've got this. Then we'll see if you can keep that dick of yours to yourself until we get to the room."

She fucking winks at me.

That does it, I think to myself before striding over to her. I slide my arm around her waist to pull her tight to me. She hides the club behind her back as if to keep it from me. But that's not what I want. I want to kiss that potty mouth of hers.

I bend close to her lips and say, "No, you've got me."

"So you're conceding the hole," she says softly, eyes heavy with desire.

"You've won."

"I have?"

"Yes, but not just this. You've won me over. And I'm not going to shank this like I did before."

"What? You're giving in on this quest to have me attend that tournament."

"No, never that. I should have told you before, but my ego got in the way. When you didn't ask me to go with you to Singapore, I thought maybe you didn't want me there."

The light in her eyes dims with confusion.

"That isn't why. I didn't want to pressure you. You have a job. Compromise and all that," she says, waving a free hand in the air.

"That's the thing. I didn't take the job with Rhoades. I decided a while ago to go at it on my own. I've been putting everything in place over the last several weeks."

"What? You changed your mind? Why?"

"You. I want to be mobile. I want to go with you to tournaments when I want. And believe me, I may not go with you to every event. But you're damn sure never flying halfway around the world again without me."

I kiss her hard and slide my hand down to the small of her back to tug her closer.

"You drive me wild, Riley."

"I do?" Her smile says she's pleased with my statement.

"You do. Ever since you walked into my life, I've been running around like a crazy man. But you've straightened out my game, made me see what's important."

"And what's that?"

"Stop playing games." Because she knows damn well what I mean.

"I just want to hear you say the words because I feel the same way."

"You're my future," I admit.

"I love you, too," she says, beating me to the punch.

"It's more than that. I love you like I've never loved another. You're my forever. Together, Eagle, we'll never hit a shanked ball again."

EPILOGUE

Pacing the room, I think about all the choices that led us to this point. Riley hasn't been feeling well, and two co-conspirators have convinced her that there can be more than one reason she's been bent over a toilet the last few days.

Both Gina and Cassie are out of town and out of my reach. Their meddling has fucked with my sex life, and Gina finds it hilarious.

Still, I mentally calculate how my finances are going. Things are moving along with my business. In fact, with Ryder and Fletcher handing out my newly minted business cards, I might be in a position to hire a few associates.

Riley's been silent behind the door. I have no idea if I should knock or wait. The answer to that question is taken out of my hands when the door opens. I watch her like a hawk for her emotions. Happy or sad? I need to know how to play this.

Downcast eyes give me a clue, but I continue to wait for her to look at me and say the words. When she does, it takes a second later before her eyes turn as bright as the smile she gives me.

"We're not pregnant?"

She launches herself into my arms on bouncing feet. She buries her face against my chest, allowing me some time to feel slightly disappointed.

For some of those long moments by myself, I've pictured a cherub-faced girl with dark hair who resembles her mother running into my arms calling me daddy. I can even see her holding a miniature golf club from practicing on the green. But my dreams haven't ended there. There is a smaller boy, a mini version of myself, though outfitted in a button-up shirt including a pocket protector carrying a calculator. Okay, so my dream isn't perfect. I'd never been a true nerd in that sense. But the family… And I'm beginning to see how ready I am for a family.

She pulls back. "Aren't you excited?"

"Yeah, sure."

Her eyes narrow. "Don't hold back on me now, Mark James."

Her use of my full name is supposed to be a threat, but it's just cute.

"Fine. Like I said before, I wouldn't mind seeing my baby grow inside of you."

I press my hand to her belly.

"So, what are you saying?"

Riley is in the prime of her career. She and I know that being pregnant will take her away from her game. And it's selfish of me not to consider that.

"I'm saying I'm a little disappointed, but I know we're not ready for it yet."

She nods. "I'll admit I might have been a little disappointed, too. Cassie has a kid. No doubt Ryder and Gina will be pregnant soon, if not already the way they go at it."

"Like us?"

Grinning, she says, "Exactly."

"Can we at least go back to no condoms?"

Having discovered the wonderful world of her pussy without them meant it had been seriously hard to go back.

"You just admitted we weren't ready to be parents. It would be irresponsible not to use them. It's double protection, me on the pill, you wearing a condom. Is it all that bad?"

"It sucks," I say, sulking.

Sliding her hand up my chest, she says, "So, if we go without and I happen to forget a pill or two, what would you do?"

That is an easy answer. "Get down on my knees and beg you to marry me."

Her eyes crinkle at the corners.

"That's what I have to do to get you to ask me?"

We haven't really talked about marriage. Our relationship is only several months old. There is so much more we need to learn about each other.

"Do you want me to ask?" Because in all honesty, why wait? What is it with people thinking that you can't fall madly in love with someone enough to marry them unless you've been together a year or so?

She bends to pick up her shoes and slide them on. When she stands up, her legs elongate, and I start to think we may not make it downstairs in time. Her eyes meet mine, and I've been caught staring at her as usual.

"I shouldn't have to tell you when to ask me," she teases.

"Yeah, thanks. A man needs a little help. No guy wants to be turned down."

"True, somehow I doubt many women have ever turned you down."

"There's a first time for everything. What would you say if I asked you?"

"I would say... I'm not telling you. But! I will tell you this. You're the only guy I've ever considered being a potential husband."

Potential. We'll work on that.

But first, she shouldn't have bothered to get dressed, because I have her naked and on her back in seconds.

It's a couple of weeks later, after Riley wins the mixed pairs tournament in New Zealand, that together, we fly back to Charlotte in time for a Valentine's Day wedding.

The weather is unusually warm that day for winter,

and the hotel has switched the indoor evening wedding to outdoors.

"That was so nice of them to suggest it," she says.

"Will you be cold?"

Because as usual, my girl wears something that seems too revealing for the amount of cloth used to design it.

"I'm fine. You would prefer I wear a muumuu."

I have no idea what that is, but it sounds like it would cover her from head to toe. "Damn right."

Unfortunately for me, she doesn't change. So as I stand across from her with a crowd beyond us, I want to bare my teeth like I have fangs for all the men who are no doubt checking her out. Her back is exposed and even on the sides, too. She insists she has some kind of tape that will keep everything hidden that should be.

Where I stand, I feel a slight breeze. I might have a little Scottish blood in me, but Gina has gone too far by making me wear a kilt. Fletcher nor Ryder is wearing one, and everyone had a good laugh at my expense when I had been informed it was no longer a joke but my reality. Something about a kilt is almost like a dress. When I balked, they all said, bride's choice. And Riley still snickers across from me, but I have a surprise for her.

At some point, I focus and listen as Ryder and Gina exchange vows. I think again about my future. There's no doubt in my mind Riley will be my wife. In fact, I want to blurt it right now. I grit my teeth to hold it back. I don't yet have a ring, and that will take some investigation to get her size.

Plus, Riley deserves me bending on one knee in grand fashion. It has to be done at some picturesque place, like on a mountain or on a beach. I want to steal her breath when I confess my deepest feelings and hopes for the future. So for now, I button up. Our time will come. This I know for sure.

As the crowd applauds for the new married pair, Fletcher and Cassie follow, and hand in hand, Riley and I take up the rear. As we parade back inside, I tug Riley off to the left as well-wishers envelop Gina and Ryder.

"Where are you taking me?" she asks.

I pull her down a short hall where I spotted a bathroom earlier. Inside, I turn the lock.

"What are you doing?" She laughs, since I haven't answered her first question.

"That damn dress," I growl while pulling up her skirt.

According to her, it's a tuxedo dress. The top resembles a vest/tuxedo, but it's cut so that if any gap appears, her breasts will be exposed to the world. That's where the tape comes in.

"See, you are the one with the sex in public thing," she says, giggling.

"It's you. You make me this way."

What I find under her skirt has me narrowing my eyes. "No panties, Eagle?"

She bites at the corner of her mouth. "Sorry, I guess I forgot."

"Forgot my ass. And you're about to find out what

real Scots wear under kilts."

Holding her skirt and managing to lift the kilt, I fist the combined fabric in one hand and hike her up with the other. "Sorry, I guess I forgot the condom. No pockets and all."

She doesn't protest, so I slide home, groaning deep and guttural.

Before desire can override us both, she says, "It's okay. I know we can get through anything together."

"You're damn right," I say, as we forget words and lose ourselves in touch and feel.

It's a good thing I'd chosen a bathroom to have my way with her in. It makes cleanup after I come like a motherfucker a lot easier.

"We should get back. They are probably taking pictures by now," she says, still grinning at how she makes me lose my mind every time I'm with her. Especially when she dresses the way she does for these formal things.

Ryder and Gina look pissed off when we join them, but it's not us they're throwing hostile glares at, but Fletcher. He looks like he snuck a cookie from the cookie jar. No doubt we'll find out later what happened.

Riley and the rest of the Wildes, including Chase, Kaycee, and her brother Landon, are taking a photo. Their dads are also in the picture. I use my phone to snap a couple. It isn't often Kaycee and Landon, Fletcher, Ryder, and Riley's cousins, come around. They grew up in Chicago and weren't always around for family get-togethers. But not everyone is here.

My sister, Andi, interrupts my thoughts. She's shocked everyone, including my parents, with her secret.

"You and Riley? I always thought it would be Gina the way you two are so close," she says.

"Gina's like another sister, you know that. And what about you? Are you seeing anyone?" When she doesn't answer, I jokingly say, "Chase and Landon aren't dating anyone."

Her smile turns into a frown, and she's ready to bolt as usual.

"No way am I dating a Wilde," she says. As she walks away, she mutters, "Never again."

Riley smiles at me from across the room, and Andi's puzzling words take a back seat to Riley's gorgeous grin.

It isn't until after Gina tosses the bouquet that I get serious time with Riley alone. I urge her to follow me outside. When we get there, it's noticeably cooler. I slip off my jacket and place it around her shoulders.

"We could have gone to the room," she pouts.

"Yeah, and we wouldn't come out again all night."

"That doesn't sound so bad."

I lick my lips because it doesn't. Still, there's something I need to say. "You know what I've been thinking all night?"

"How you're going to get me off again."

Sliding my finger down her nose, I say, "That's a given. But there."

I point to the small platform where Gina and Ryder

stood. It's done up with flowers and lights strung above.

"What about it?"

"I thought about how gorgeous you're going to be on our wedding day."

God, her smile makes her one in a million. Her father got a kick out of me thanking him for basically having sex with his wife that eventually created his daughter. I think I got away with it because I grew up with their family. I've always been around. And when we were younger, all of us boys would say all kinds of things to their dads.

Riley gains my attention back with her reply, "Is that so?"

"It is. I've told you before you're my forever girl, and I mean it. Though we aren't ready for that step tonight, mainly because I don't have a ring yet, forever starts somewhere. What I do have is this."

I may not have had a pocket or a condom, but I did have a sporran, the equivalent of a man purse that went with the kilt getup. From it, I remove a long loop of ribbon. Attached to it is a key.

"I don't want to spend another night or another morning without you in my arms. This is a key to my place, but I don't care where we live as long as we live together."

"What's the ribbon for?"

"The better to tie you up later," I say, giving her a little wink. "But you haven't answered me. Will you move in with me?"

Her eyes grow and fill. "If you mean it, yes."

"I do, and I promise you that you will be my wife one day."

Her hand reaches up and pulls my face to hers. The kiss is so damn powerful everything goes dark.

She giggles. "Someone turned off the lights."

"We can go back inside," I say, holding her in my arms under the glow of moonlight.

"It doesn't matter as long as I'm with you. Today has been perfect, the best Valentine's ever." She presses her lips to mine in a quick kiss. "I love you, Mark James."

"I love you, Riley James." I lick my lips, testing out the name.

"I like the sound of that."

"So do I," I say.

Under the moonlit sky, our next kiss feels like forever. Tonight, we take the first steps into a lifetime together.

Her eyes linger on mine as she struggles to speak.

"You have to know I didn't think a relationship was ever in my future." A tear spills from her eye. I wipe it away with my thumb. She smiles, composing herself. "I'd written off men so long ago. But you made me a believer again."

I dip my head and nip at her lip, which gains me another giggle from her. Too soon, I'll be looking for another hidey-hole to find my way inside her again.

"You obliterated my world when you walked into it. I'd be a broken man without you."

Her eyes are full of mirth. "Just admit it. You got

shanked!"

   She winked at me.

   And I'm man enough to say it. "I most certainly did."

THE END

A THANK YOU

We'd like to thank you for taking the time out of your busy life to read our novel. Above all we hope you loved it. If you did, we would love it back if you could spare just a few more minutes to leave a review on your favorite retailer. If you do, could you be so kind and not leave any spoilers about the story? Thanks so much!

ACKNOWLEDGEMENTS

To every athlete out there, who dedicates hours and hours to their sport, we thank you and appreciate you. Not only do you entertain us, but you also give us something to write (fantasize) about!

To our readers: you guys are THE BEST! And we say that from the bottoms of our hearts. We love and appreciate each and every one of you and we hope our little dirty, flirty romance is something that you love. We decided to play a little with this and veer away from the serious so we could have some fun. So please tell us what you think. Hit us up on Facebook or wherever, but there will be more Wilde Players on the way.

Here are the lovely people we'd like to say THANK YOU to. Our beta readers: Kristie, Andrea, Nina, and Jill. You ladies are our shining stars and always make our books brighter and prettier than they can ever have been without you. We Love you to the end zone and then some!

Thank you Nina Grinstead, and Social Butterfly PR for running your butt off in getting our stuff out there when we were so late. We love you!

And thank you Rick Miles at Redcoat PR For everything, but especially for putting up with Annie (and Walter) after two pots of coffee. Next time she'll just give the coffee to Walter.

STALK A.M. HARGROVE

If you would like to hear more about what's going on in my world, please subscribe to my mailing list at http://amhargrove.com/mailing-list/.

Please stalk me. I'll love you forever if you do. Seriously.

Website: www.amhargrove.com

Twitter: @ amhargrove1

Facebook Page:/ AMHargroveAuthor

Facebook:/ anne.m.hargrove

Goodreads:/ amhargrove1

Instagram: @ amhargroveauthor

Pinterest:/ amhargrove1

annie@amhargrove.com